The President's APOCALYPSE PROPHECY

Optimum Vizh-an

Order this book online at www.trafford.com
or email orders@trafford.com

Most Trafford titles are also available at major online book retailers.

Print information available on the last page.

ISBN: 978-1-4907-7472-5 (sc)
ISBN: 978-1-4907-7471-8 (e)

Trafford rev.   06/27/2016

Trafford
PUBLISHING®   www.trafford.com
North America & international
toll-free: 1 888 232 4444 (USA & Canada)
fax: 812 355 4082

Contents

unedited manuscript

*This unedited manuscript is by no means
an anti-government and or anti-establishment
prophecy. It is a possible fore sight
of what the US Government System might be like
in the United States of America's future.
If not, then more like the back drops,
to a Science Fiction movie.*

Dedication

This book is dedicated
to all of us who love to serve others,
regardless of how challenging
our personal hardships are.

In every selfless act I did,
I showed you *Unconditional Love*
and with this kind of persistent work,
we must help the self-centered weak,
while remembering the words of
Christ himself said:
*'It is more blessed to give
than to receive.'"*

ACTS 20:35
New Friendship Bible

Author

Habakkuk

Then the LORD replied:
"Write down the revelation
and make it plain on tablets
so that a herald may run with it.
For the revelation awaits
an appointed time;
it speaks of it's manifestation
and will prove not self-centered.
Though it linger,
wait for it;
it will certainly come
and will not delay.

Habakkuk 2:2-3
New Friendship Bible

Disclaimer

This book has no connection and or affiliation whatsoever with the man called Donald Trump, his logos, his companies, his employees, etc. This book was not created for the purpose of promoting Donald Trump, Donald Trump's estates, the Donald Trump 2016 Presidential Campaign, and or anything else in association with Donald Trump. Including all those associated with Donald Trump's family, his businesses and or non-business associates.

The words "Donald Trump" is used as a definition description, referenced to a type of person who can minimize collateral damage, of financial decisions that made sense at the moment; but in time, due to a new series of continual negative circumstances, the original financial commitment becomes obsolete. The sooner the intervention occurs, the sooner the leftover assets can be used to build a new foundation of wealth; for its customers / clients / citizens.

There are two reasons why these words were used together in describing this financial recycling process. The first is due to the urgency in recycling obsolete financial decisions, from the past centuries. There is no time to waste in creating, building and propagating a new word from scratch, which describes this technique / solution; that minimizes and or prevents complete financial devastating lost to its clients / consumers / citizens. Second, we're at an all time high in the "there's no turning back" statuses for government and corporation bubbles around the world; ready to burst wide open.

These two I.C.U. Emergencies warrant the use of a word and or words that everyone can associate with now, versus sometime in the future, when perhaps it will be too late to apply. This logic is based on the classic example; most crowds can associate with when someone yells in a fearful tone, "FIRE!" inside a packed building. Everyone in that room, who heard those bone chilling words, understands the dire need of finding an escape route ASAP! The people who heard the word "FIRE!" with undivided captive attention, are more than likely thinking, "Is this real?" while looking for the nearest exit. Visually verifying, by how the crowd is responding, the smells in the atmosphere and acts accordingly. *This example is based on a real fire and not someone miss using the word "fire!" for prank purposes.*

This prophecy has no connection with Kim Clement and or Kim Clement Ministries, who have referenced future events associated and or alluding to with the key words "Trump", "Trumpet", etc; located in his online data base at kimclement.com /prophecy.php.

If any of this prophecy does come true; it is only coincidental and should be considered as an inspiration for better days to come.

For those of us who bought this book in hopes of reading a prophecy on Donald Trump the man, who is running for and or did run for President in 2016; pending the time this book is read, here we go…

This is for entertainment purposes only and should be received as such, by individuals and media outlets.

Donald Trump will win the November Election 2016 and become the 45th President of the US. He will set in motion the retooling of the US Government to meet the needs of the 21st Century, with Zero Overhead as targeted budgets. This will prevent any type of establishment from re-infecting itself back into any of the recycled government entities. This retooling will be commonly referred to as US Gov 2.0, USA2.0 and or the US Government Reformation Era.

The establishments, infected in various entities, will fight back as hard as they can. But every time they do, they will lose their hypnotic grip while observing its self crumbling before its very own eyes; like dead trees in a raging forest fire.

This country was erected by God's mercy from day one, for His purposes alone. Just because humans can manipulate a few resources, doesn't mean they are the final authority on what they can not see.

There will be those who will sit back and witness His Merciful Glory. Others will have no clue with what's going on and will take what ever they can; based on their self-centrism and insecurities.

The temptation will be great for Donald Trump to run for a second term, but he will not. He will establish as a Constitutional Amendment that the Presidents preceding him and other government officials; can only serve for no more than 4 years, per office title. He will lead by example during this Reformation period of the US Government.

Donald Trump will set motion the undoing of most of what the 44th President established through executive order. He will go onto adding more to the United States of America then what was accomplished over the last 100 yrs, within 4yrs of his term as President; with the people, through the people and by the people. He will give all the credit to the people for what they accomplished as a nation.

Donald Trump will be noted in the US Government history books, as the Father of the US Government Reformation Era Period.

Note: Prophecy is the ability in seeing glimpses into anything that currently appears to be questionable, with no current tangible proof to prove it; to be as so. Prophecy's intentions are to bring peace to those who want to understand how to navigate through the challenges, they are confronting with from time to time.

Disclaimer for me: Just because I pen this prophecy, doesn't mean I am voting for and or supporting the man named Donald Trump, who is running for and or did run for President in 2016, with the anticipation of expecting this Donald Trump, to be the Father of the US Government Reformation Era Period. He might not be this "Donald Trump" type of person who is needed to recycle these ready to burst bubbles.

If this man Donald Trump, who gets elected in 2016 as President of the United States, does nothing like the previous Presidents, who have created and added to the various Government entity bubbles, then there will be another person who will be running with a different name, but will be a "Donald Trump" type person. It could be even a woman. This man Donald Trump running for and or did run for the 2016 Presidential race could be a plant from the establishment, in hopes of dissipating the people's frustrations only to buy more time in infecting the various USA Government entities. If so, the people who are tired of the US Government not doing what they say, they will get even angrier; to the point of physically organizing an internal revolution. Not a revolution with guns and bullets, but a revolution of subdividing the current fifty states into newer states. These newer states would instantaneously shed themselves from their former debt ridden state entities. This was a common, accepted evolutionary process of the USA in her earlier history. These newer state entities would start out debt free and become the most desirable new states to live in, obtain jobs and retire in. This type of revolution would be the incubator in producing masses of people, abandoning these "older" states suffocating with debt, for a better life and have "a say" in their new state governments. *Similar to the mass placement of people moving from the East Coast to the West Coast, in California Gold Rush years.* The current debt ridden states would go bankrupt. The "Donald Trump" type people and organizations would step in and recycle these bankrupt state size ghetto entities.

It is expected that this prophecy, like all other prophecies will be scrutinized by the nay sayers, historians and religious elite; for its authenticity and accuracy.

So instead of waiting for it to happen, let's dive into this now. No secrets hiding in the closet here, no cover up conspiracies and or no waiting for the interviews that may never happen on prime time; to better explain this prophecy.

Does the author qualify? Nope. This is just a personal vision that I penned and I was able to publish this vision for a few hundred dollars; thanks to digital publishing with Trafford Publishing. Trafford Publishing does an awesome job in creating the venue for anyone to become a published author. This basic book package gets anyone in over 450 plus web stores; including in the big brand name stores and in over 30 plus countries. Great people! Greater is the Team! *And I highly recommend them to anyone who wants to publish the book of their dreams! Note:* This package offering was purchased in 2015.

Back in the 90's I thought Trump would make a good President. But since I didn't publically state it on Name Brand News Medias over and over, until it was common knowledge, it's worthless to anyone and everyone who wants to reads it now. *Most will more than likely say that I made that reference up as a way of self anointing myself.* Nope. Don't give a rip, if any of this prophecy comes true.

God lets whatever happens, happen, as He sees fit. His ways are far above my ways. He can make life out of anything, at anytime, from where ever He chooses. He is not restricted by man's choices, time and or space.

Do the parts of this prophecy, that don't come true, disqualify the whole prophecy? Nope. I see my vision in part. I'm describing it the best I can, from how I see it now versus living in it 24/7 somewhere in the future. Then coming back in time and describing it to the tee.

Did the author craft this prophecy just to get fifteen minutes of fame? Nope. If Media Networks find this, please do not be tempted to cover this prophecy, due to current events that are occurring and or if this is being researched later in the 21st century and beyond, for it's accuracy. This prophecy is a personal vision from my puny prospective of life, while standing on tiny speck of dirt, in this huge universe. However, more than likely the media will use this, for their fifteen minutes of fame.

Note: Medias only exist if they can get people's attention. So they try really hard to find those fifteen minutes of fame stories and sequentially air them in hopes of creating an audience. The larger the audience, the higher they can charge for advertising on their channel. They have the greater temptation of finding fifteen minutes fame stories then I do. They're addicted to catering to as many people as they can; in hopes of finding their next big story, to expand on for weeks to come, if not months. These sequential fifteen minutes to fame stories are the life blood to their entity. They know the weaker these fifteen minutes to fame stories are, the weaker their blood and heart is. So their strength depends on finding as many of the juiciest fifteen minutes to fame stories as they can. If they can't, their temptation will be to conjure up their own, even if it means sacrificing their own employees. When this happens, it's defiantly a clear sign, that this entity is infected with an establishment.

For those who like to minimize, distort and distract vision, they can easily say I have watched too many sci-fi movies over my life time. And have collaborated them altogether to create this prophecy, based on all their concepts mixed together. My short response back is, anyone can make a potshot from a snapshot. However, to the best of my ability, this documented prophecy is original and the first compilation of its kind. This is why it has been copyrighted and published for entertainment purposes.

Added thoughts to keep in remembrance:

1. People of all walks of life, beliefs and cultures are tempted to conjure up conspiracies, when their world becomes the darkest and their "end" looks closer.
2. Those people who are looking for hope tend to gravitate to these conspiracists.
3. Conspiracies only become real, especially to its believers, during those darkest hours in human history.
4. Let's all do ourselves a big favor and remember History is "His Story" not ours.

Preface
Two Part Preface: First Part.

Welcome to one of those moments in history, where history makes a defining change in geo-political alignments...*if we like it or not.*

This is not a book on a few one liner prophecies about Donald Trump, the man himself, that's backed up with a bunch more of prophecies unrelated but used to justify why these few one liners on Donald Trump are going to be true as well. Like those who go around and say, I prophecy this and this and this and this and they all came true, so therefore this will come true as well. The long lists of unrelated prophecies that continually come true promote more of that prophet(s) and create a fan base versus tangible workable applications. Not condemning this "type" of prophecy; it's just more of form of encouragement to those who are desperately looking for hope to hang on and a warning to those who are addicted to suppressing people.

This prophecy book provides tons of insights and wisdom that will allow the individual, communities, cities, nations and galaxies to build their wealth, health and legacies; while minimizing huge loses due to these defining moments in history, from now to the end of time.

This *President's Apocalypse prophecy* goes to the core of why these tyrannist corporate entities have become exceedingly great and powerful and the types of people, who bring these empires crashing down, while others recycle them.

This prophetic logic is the same for most of, if not all of recent history's major events.

Regardless of the culture, social-economic status and religion; we all seeking a "safe" routine to live our "normal" lives in. Little knowingly find out we're that frog that's sitting in the frying pan, which someone else has been slowly turning up the heat on. It's so slow we don't know the difference. We're fed daily and appear to be safe, so what's the rush? Then one day, we realize we are paralyzed by death; slowly cooked to death and didn't even know it. This is how most major events become all of a sudden in our face real. The hidden self-centered agenda of tyrannist corporate entities is now as clear as a sunny day. Who could have of seen the dark clouds in the distance; to have planned their days better? Maybe a few people in that whole crowd were fortunate enough to see it. As they speak, it's gibberish (prophecy and or revelation) to everyone else who can't see it. As time passes, it becomes more relevant. Stories of people becoming innocent victims are apart of everyday conversations. Bam! Lightening and thunder introduces the final act of death and destruction to the masses, who did not heed the warnings. Entities are decimated overnight.

Here are some of those moments that have been captured by pen in our past, to help remind us that this is more than likely not gibberish:

Goliath met his David. In all his established glory, he envisioned the Israelites being their nation's slaves. He's over 9 feet tall, full of brawn and covered in heavy metal armor. Israel was at her wits end. Even the conventional metal weaponry seemed pale in comparison, to this giant's tyrannical empire had acquired; and now is justifying decimating Israel's kingdom authority, so that it can expand its own. Israel gripped in fear. Goliath consumed with self-centrism, provokes the nation of Israel. In this pinnacle moment, history brings to the fore front a little sheppard boy. Scrawny in stature, non compliant to the status quo and more than likely illegitimate; both nations infected with an establishment was in denial that this little scrawny boy was going to change the coarse of both their nations. David grabs five smooth stones and embeds the first into Goliath's forehead; then the other four into Goliath's brother's fore heads. Both establishments in both conflicting nations were decimated in a few moments with five stones. Goliath's nation runs in fear as the people of that nation saw their establishment crumbling before their very own eyes. Israel's governing establishment saw they lost control of convincing their people, they were in charge. Israel was now being governed by a little scrawny boy, who was using a simple but powerful new form of weaponry. David's scrawniness was mistaken for weakness.

Goliath's Obsession: Big Heavy Armor. *Dismantled by:* Simple, light weight armor; with higher speed and accuracy.

Satan met his Christ. In all of Satan's self-centered wisdom, believes now he can take advantage of Christ foolishly laying his life down for "sinners". He thrashes Christ's body through the Jewish Sanhedrin and Pilate's Roman henchman. A few days ago, Christ was being welcomed as the new deliverer for the suppressed people by both Israel and Rome. The self-centered establishments of both nations desperately conspired Christ's death to maintain their very own self-centered lives. After hanging on a cross, marred beyond all human recognition, like road kill on a stick; after hanging on for three hours on a cross, Christ chooses to give up his own life. See *New Friendship Bible, Optimum Vizh-an, Trafford Publishing.* Satan had Christ right where he wanted him, in hell; his domain, his rules and his foolishness. His self-centerism is at an all time high was his undoing. Christ appearing to be marred beyond all recognition. As John the Baptist announced decimation to their current establishments of Israel and Rome, with "Behold the lamb/deliverer of God" so now in Hell to Satan. Fear and loneliness grips Satan's heart, for the very first time of his life. All the fear he had inflicted on mankind, since mankind giving up their place in the garden, to this point combined is now falling on him. Christ gazing into the depths of Satan's eyes with compassion and mercy, only takes the keys of Satan's established authority over Hell. Satan's self-centered establishment was decimated. Satan helplessly looks on as Christ sets free all those who hungered to be by God's side on resurrection day. Christ's compassion was mistaken for weakness.

Satan's Obsession: Death to Life. *Dismantled by:* Life to Death.

Persians met their Alexander the Great. Persian's self-centered establishment was now justifying its need in expanding their kingdom in the direction of Europe. Alexander saw the predictability of the Persians putting more faith in their routine war tactics versus being able to adjust to random attack tactics. The Persian establishment mistakenly took Alexander's youth as a weakness. Alexander would command his out number forces into groups large enough, to deceive the Persian forces to veer from their normal attack routines; long enough to split them up thinly at key points. Alexander repeatedly did this successfully without the Persian army ever figuring this out. Each time it was a different game plan but he used the same tactical logic.

Persian's Obsession: Decisiveness and Technology. *Dismantled by:* Rights to Incision and Prosperity.

China met their Genghis Khan. China's establishment rested on the ideology that no outsiders would ever rule over China. Genghis Khan's small raids were perceived as pettiness. Using these tactics on the key strongholds of China, all of China fell into the hands of Genghis Khan. Genghis Khan engineered a nice long list of firsts, which were used to outwit the Chinese and other nations as well. Long list here we go… he: granted religious freedom before anyone else adopted it, Christians Muslims Buddhists fought side by side for Genghis Khan, abolished torture, encourage trade, united nomadic tribes, warriors in groups of ten, abolished inherited aristocratic titles, forbad selling and kidnapping women, writing system, choose competent allies versus relatives in key positions, army had no supply train or reserves, a postal system – yes you read that right – a postal system. That's not what I was taught in the public school. Shame on you public school system; now write on the chalk board 100 times, "I will teach the truth about Genghis Khan." And the best is for last, he was the first to create his signature tactic move – the false withdrawal then bam a siege.

China's Obsession: Invincible to Foreigners. *Dismantled by:* Competitive Engineering.

Aztecs met their Cortes. Aztec's establishment rested their existence on making the war god happy, by human sacrifice. Their winning wars were based their rituals to the war god; in hopes of making him happy. If so they won, if not they lost. Cortes comes along with his Christian beliefs of unconditional forgiveness. No rituals needed to appease the gods. Cortes appeased his God through asking forgiveness of his selfishness. Then oops, Cortes introduces Smallpox to the Aztecs with no known cure. It's fitting how the Aztecs sow the seed of human sacrifice and then Smallpox comes along and wipes out 20 to 30% of Aztec population. Cortes wants to introduce to them the concept that asking for the forgiveness of their selfishness appeases the God of all gods versus all that on going waste of human lives through sacrificing.

Aztec's Obsession: Appeasing gods. *Dismantled by:* Unconditional forgiveness.

The Holy Roman Empire met its Napoleon Bonaparte. The Holy Roman Empire's establishment is based on all countries are under the leadership of one leader; like Christ is over the church. Napoleon's desire was to incorporate within the people's heart; their right to liberty, equality and fraternity within the concept of nationalism. With Napoleon's strengths; at being the fastest in moving armies from one location to the other and injecting war propaganda in communications media at key moments during his military campaigns, he was able to show the people its possible.

The Holy Roman Empire's Obsession: Micro Managing Continental Unity. *Dismantled by:* Individualism.

South Africa met its Nelson Mandela. South Africa's establishment institutionalized the separation of race, based on the color of human skin. Apartheid. Laws were put in place to enforce the separation of race at the local level; imprisonment, torturing plus extra fines and taxes. One race is receiving a ton more privileges, without paying for them. While the other race is paying a ton more; and receiving none and or very little benefits. As Mandela personally experiences this with his under privileged race, showed his people how to stand up for their individual rights and defend their rights as a collective whole. His greatest messages and support to his race came from his 27 yrs of imprisonment. His race overcame, shut down Apartheid and Nelson Mandela was elected President of South Africa.

Apartheid's Obsession: Race Separation. *Dismantled by:* Collective Value.

The 20ᵗʰ Century Corporate Tyrannist met their Donald Trump. Say what? What does a Donald Trump have to do with Corporate Tyrannist? And how in history's name does a Donald Trump even come close in comparing to these greats of our past? Fair question. Self-centered corporate tyrannist establishments have infected governing entities to expand their domain; in all forms of governments throughout the world. *Corporations were designed to be by the people and for the people, not for an inner circle of a small group of self-centered people or family;* be it formed in capitalism, socialism, communism and even the fascist regimes of rouge terrorist entities. The life blood of these governing entities have been coming from these 20ᵗʰ century self-centered tyrant corporate entities. A "Donald Trump" person will look at these entities that have been infected with an establishment, in the same way failing businesses audit themselves to make the necessary changes to survive. An honest accurate audit reveals the real efficiencies of the different components of the business. What is effective and what is not effective. People can't argue with that, so overall the *"audit process" is a form of compassion*. It gently warns those who are being inefficient to get their act together in making the changes to be efficient asap. As the masses see the benefits of this approach, the audit process will accelerate to other entities.

Corporate Tyrannist Obsession: Self-Centered god like Status. *Dismantled by:* Unconditional Compassion.

Preface
Two Part Preface: Second Part.

So… here we are at crossroads of another defining moment in history. We can reason away most everything, most of the time. But when major events super impose their presence on us, they're in our faces relentlessly. No matter how far we go to avoid them, they find us, corner us and then try to steal away all of our hope in believing for better days ahead.

Should we keep heading straight on Day Dreamers Freeway aka DD Hwy to Denial City? Some of us will go to the death of our self-centerism before we open our eyes, to what is really happening. Life is bigger than who I think I am.

Should we take a left on Paranoia Avenue to Conspiracists Theme Park? This is like being in half denial and half realists but never making a commitment to either or. I get twitchy when something bad happens to me so then I invest in time to protect myself and my loved ones. When skies are blue in between the bad events then I thing "everything" is ok.

Or should we take a right on the Real Deal Highway to Hunkerdowns Campgrounds? This is like, Oh _____ fill in the blank moment. My stomach is tied in knots and I'm heading for the fetal position real fast. During the blue sky moments, I catch up on my sleep that I lost the last three weeks worrying day and night, thinking of a contingency plan. Feeling rested, I come to my senses in wanting to save my life and my loved ones. We make serious cut backs, down size the home, stop the bennies, and move to a more stable home environment to wait out the storm. If my job is working on thin ice, I squeeze in acquiring a skill trade versus relying on my framed college certificate of "something important" hanging on my walls of fantasy living.

Regardless of our Culture, Race and or Religion, when these major events happen, they stop us dead in our tracks and force us to make new "no turning back" life decisions. I can be making a deeper commitment to any of the three general categories above, or abruptly changing my course. The longer I wait the lesser options I have to choose form. Either or when I draw the line on the bottom of what ever I choose and add it up, it equals a life changing moment in my life.

With all this background info, let's press into a tangible seeable understanding mechanics of what's behind creating all this chaos that "abruptly" clings to us with the intent of destroying us and our loved ones. And if we're fortunate enough to shake it loose; maybe clean up the mess and build a better world for our families to live in…

The President's Apocalypse prophecy goes to the core of what creates these life changing events. So that we can learn how to cut our lost, recycle our bad decisions and build a better life for ourselves, our families and our communities; no matter what age or century we live in.

The core of this prophecy is in reference to the effect and out come of tangible and intangible bubbles that are created by self-centered tyrannist entities, which enviably burst over time, due to the weakness of the bubbles walls.

If we all live long enough, sooner or later we see all the markets max out, implode and adjust their scales of economy up or down; based on it's *new **actual*** customer supply and demand. No matter how much forced regulation is put on consumers to guarantee sales with the updated versions, controlling supply and demand, and or manipulation of economies of scale, all are used to sustain an entity's market's growth; all these bubbles will pop. Guaranteed!

This truth also soberly applies to intangible entities as well. These intangible entities are rarely talked about in main stream media, such as: educational institutions, service industries and government bureaucracies. Yes. Government entities have bubbles that will burst too. How? It happens when a government chooses to cease serving and protecting its citizens at minimal cost, for expanding its unlimited and unaccountable bureaucracy controls on its citizens, to better serve and protect its career politicians.

Donald Trump, as in the man, has personally made decisions that have created wealth. Then a series of uncontrollable negative financial events occurred that destroyed his wealth. Versus giving up, he recycled what was left and built it into a new foundation of wealth within a short period of time. This personal experience qualifies and confirms he has the cognitive skills, to recycle previous financial commitments into successfully at or near zero cost to its customers. *This does not guarantee he will be able to do this again in the future and or on a larger scale,* but better describes the definition of what type of solution, that is needed to limit the financial collateral damage to its clients, customers and citizens; caused by these bursting bubbles.

The character of this "Donald Trump" type person will more than likely not conform to a particular race, culture and or religion. They will appear reckless, repulsive and uncommitted. But when left alone, they work what appears to be "miracles" to those who are trying to do everything "right" versus being effective.

In summary, the two words "Donald Trump" is in the context of an individual and or team of individuals having the cognitive skills to make sober decisions, that will prevent bubbles from being created and neglected or even near long term zero costs, to that entity and it customers/citizens. Another words, having the ability to recycle previous financial commitments; into at and or near zero long term financial repercussions to its customers and citizens.

A person who can do this is called a "Donald Trump" and a group of people who do this are called "Donald Trumpers."

With this preface presented, let us now see what these "Donald Trumps/Trumpers" will do in the future to minimize the effects of these bursting bubbles to its clients, customers and citizens.

This prophecy is for those of us who find ourselves living; in the midst of a neglected, exhausted governmental, educational and or large economies of scale entities. Their bubbles are or will be bursting soon and we're realizing we might be on verge of and or are losing everything we've worked, so very hard for.

Problem: Establishment

Any past, present and or future Establishments attempting to harness a country's government, for the sole purpose of meeting their self interests to further their self gain, only serve themselves and not the people of that government. If an establishment gets footing within any governing body then that establishment will need to continue to manipulate and regulate its citizens, to gain further control; with their intent to increase their personal assets, fame and influence. *A governing body is created to serve the people, not for the people to serve the governing body.*

Genocide seems to be a huge precursor that marks the dramatic turning points in history. One culture leader is bent on eradicating the weak and or innocent of a neighboring town, state, country and or nation. After the genocide attempt is made, ironically that infraction becomes non-existent. Those who were isolated for extinction, now become the established and well influential people of their town(s), state(s), country(s) and or nation(s). Examples: 20th century Jews were isolated by Hitler to be removed from the face of the earth. Shortly afterwards, it is Hitler that was removed from the face of the earth and Germany split in two nations. Then Jews got their own nation and become technological blessing to all the nations of the earth. Ironically about 2000 yrs before this, a predominate man: statesman, Pharisee of Pharisees, knowing thoroughly all of the scriptures and more than likely having the highest odds in liberating the Jews from Roman rule; was bent on eradicating all the Christians, with full blessings from the Jewish people. This guy wrote the play book for Hitler and ISIS. His name was Saul of Tarsus. His exterminations went off without a glitch. Nothing could stop him. It was as though he felt he was doing God's will, because God wasn't stopping him. *Oops.* That's when He did. His road to Damascus encounter; took a non-stop killing machine, all in the name of God and made this Saul of Tarsus mercifully into Paul; who lived on and wrote ¾'s of the New Testament. This Jewish territory goes on to be trashed and put into non-existences for about 1850 plus years. Whereas the Christians flourish all over the earth; splitting the Roman Empire in two, country's throughout the earth witness in their history for a season liberating transformation, the longest being the United States of America. If history holds true to this course, then ISIS will shortly become non-existent and more than likely become Christian for several centuries to come; with Islam and its divisions becoming the undesirable minority, throughout the earth. The threats of IRAN of annihilating ISRAEL, well more than likely transform into making Israel a Formable Super Power in her region and throughout the earth, for centuries to come. And IRAN will soberly become "I RAN" in shame for even thinking of genociding ISRAEL. And humbly becoming a predominate Major Christian Nation in the region for centuries to come as well.

These are a couple of examples of former governing entities that became infected with an establishment. When the establishment reached a saturation level within the entity, it had to reach outside the entity to consume other entities to continue its existence. When Saul reached saturation level within the Sanhedrin to continue his existence, he had to consume the Christians. When Hitler reached saturation level within Germany, he had to consume the Jews living within Germany to gain complete control of Germany then turning his hunger to foreign nations. Etc...

Take the above examples and apply the same logic to all the other entities that are hungry to grow and expand at the expense of other entities. It never changes. Well ok at least until God's final decision, in Progensis. *New Friendship Bible.*

Defined

The word *establishment* in this prophecy manuscript is defined as a person, group of people and or a network of entities that work in unison, for the betterment of themselves versus its clients, customers and or citizens; whom say they're serving. Those dedicated to and within the establishment, can be outwardly appearing to those who they "serve" as working together in unison and or in contrary, but internally "behind closed doors" are working for the same cause.

In other words, the establishment is a modern day form of pirates 2.0 pillaging its clients, customers and or citizens while reassuring their clients, customers and or citizens with promises and guarantees its ok. Pirates of 1.0 have turned in their pirate flags, wooden legs and metal hook hands into Pirates 2.0 versions of polyester suits and CEO suites. Examples: Establishment leaders could be of trusted corporations and institutions, the whole corporation itself, governing bodies, media outlets, lifetime health maintenance programs with no intention of curing, etc. The establishment can be formed from any one of these entities and or any combination of all of these entities. Anyone of these entities can be completely clueless that an establishment has taking it over.

The establishment can infect any form of government; democracy, fake democracy, socialism, fascism; any culture, religious ritual societies, and clan; any city, state, country; alliances of any of the above plus. If there is a network of any kind, then the establishment has the potential to infect it. The establishment is like a parasite; a blood leach on the human skin, a tapeworm in the bowels of a mammal, a tick on dog, a barnacle on a whale. A parasite lives off the provider, at the provider's expense and gives nothing in return. *Comparison Examples:* Empty campaign speeches, benefits given to non-tax payers, over priced appliances, worthless diplomas, maintenance drugs that are later replaced because of side effects, etc.

Until the establishment is terminated, the establishment will continue to infect its chosen entity, until the entity is completely consumed.

Parasites are known to change the appearance and behavior of its host, without the host comprehending it; so it is with establishments. The establishment is the human design of a parasite entity. There are parasites in the plant and animal kingdoms. Establishments are the parasites of the human entity kingdom. As the establishment infects its chosen entity, it produces a "gas" that inflates the entities expenses; or another words expensive solutions that produce very little benefits, if not nothing at all, for the clients, customers and or citizens in which the entity they desire to be apart of.

Another good comparison is the Venus Fly Trap plant. It displays its seductive mixture of aromas and taste that lures its prey into its domain/system/life and then turns on its prey, closes its mouth and begins to digest its latest victim. The Venus Fly Trap does not give its food out the kindness of its heart; it comes with dire conditions. While other plants give their food away to anyone who is interested to take it as desired; with "no strings" attach, per say.

The establishment thrives off a set of predictable routines. It demands a specific routine to be kept, to keep its sanity. If the routine is broken; threats of personal lost are made, intimidation and coercion are common communicational techniques. It continues it's on going cycle of controlled choke holds over its clients/customers/citizens, until it has drained all life from its victims. It doesn't do this all at once, or it would be noticed by all those who pass by. Its goal is to do this as slow as possible and take the longest possible time. For the establishment knows when the entity has been completely infected and has been completely drained of all life, it to will die.

Note: This is not a prophecy against establishments. This is explanation of how bubbles grow to the point of bursting.

Routines as described as double edged swords in the book *Can My Life Change,* Author: Optimum Vizhan, with Trafford Publishing. *Routines are double edged swords. On one side of the blade, it cuts through the distractions of obtaining our goals. The other side convinces us there is no other way to forge ahead. A routine gradually hypnotizes us into believing that our deliverance comes from it. All routines end results make us complacent. It's not being at the right place, at the right time.* **God is everywhere** and *never limited to a pattern. A continual sequence pattern produces a routine. The key is in breaking the self induced routine trance. Self inflected trances by my own patterns. Patterns offer false securities of being ok. Unplanned fast, breaks a feeding routine. Eating a new food group changes a nutritional routine. A new subject changes a study routine. Moving the furniture around in a room, changes a view routine. Job change status changes a work routine. Getting married, changes a life style routine. Having a child changes a relationship routine...*

In the moments of my doubts, I try to reach out into believing God can change my life; even though I have no clue how He will, I ask give me the faith and the will to believe, it can. The moment between my hardship routine and those thoughts that consume my mind and heart, to when the hope manifests; is faith growing in the midst of my confusion.

The establishment will resist, sacrifice its own and use religious leaders to validate its right to exist. As long as the status quo doesn't bring the establishment into accountability, the establishment will grow in arrogance with more regulations and imply death threats to those who do not follow through, with the oaths of alliance. When the status quo begins to attack the establishment, it will use all forms of media to openly discredit those who are attacking it.

The sign that the establishment's bubble is about to burst and cease to exist will be, when majority of the time the establishment attacks, it will suffer lost, it will not be able to recoup the lost and its descending cycle will continue, until it no longer exists. The same toxic fumes that lured its new supporters in will now become the toxic fumes that dismantle the establishment by confusion, betrayal and influence.

Everyone can justify their means as to why they make and stick to the decisions, commitments and abandonments, they believe in. *There is a way that seems right to a self-centered man, but in the end it leads to his loneliness.* Prov 16:25. *New Friendship Bible.* So it is with establishments. Since establishments are created by self-centered individual(s) conspiring to gain control of an entity, so to the establishment(s).

People either find peace in being friends with God, living an honorable life and or being self-center. Any one of these types of peace is true and real to the person, who justifies their actions, to attain it. So it is with establishments. Since establishments are created by self-centered individuals(s), so to the establishments can be at and or searching for peace; as it infects its victim entity.

Self-Centered

Self-centered is as in every thought, every move, every decision, every interconnection, every motive to accomplish a desired self-centered goal; all for oneself, without any intentions of sharing; is self-centerism at its finest. Self-Centerism covers up its selfishness with justifiable intentions. Self-Centerism will sacrifice anything and anyone to attain its goal. It will lie while it lies and waits for days, for years, for centuries if need be, to attain its goal. To maximize the control of its Self-Centerism, it will seek leadership roles; choosing clueless victims with low self-esteem, that will feel guilty for not following this type of leader. Others will ignorantly befriend themselves with this type of leader, thinking it will get them to the "top" quicker, when in reality they will become escape goats for the Self-Centered leaders. Self-Centerism is minutely calculated, more dedicated and more determined to obtain its goals, then any other force known to mankind.

Self-Centerism subtly repeats the same logical cycle, habitually until it reaches its goals.

This is Self-Centerism's Normal cycle:

1. Act of Kindness.
2. Form of Bonding.
3. Creates Artificial conflict.
4. Blames victim.
5. Uses Acts of Kindness to Justify.
6. Verbal, Physical and or Financial Abuses.
7. Leaves.
8. Apologizes to Restart Cycle.

With all of that, in regards to an establishment infecting an entity, the establishment infects the entity, by doing the following. 1. Offers what appears to be a no strings attached benefit to its personal / clients / customers / citizens. Once the desired recipient(s) have appeared to genuinely received their benefit(s) then… 2. Communicates to recipient(s) the desire to bond through friendship, marriage, partnerships, etc... Once recipient(s) verbally and or physically consents, with this "new" found love/friendship, then 3. A calculated conflict is created, from what ever has recently transpired. *A seed turned into an instant thorn bush; from anything that is logical to un-logical.*

If nothing is available to act upon, then something will be misplaced and or taken, with intent to turn the fake event into a thorn bush… Once the recipient(s) have justified it was a miss understanding, then 4. The recipient(s) are blamed for the trust bond between them to be broken. No matter on much the recipient(s) reason they didn't do it, the establishment will use the fake event as guilty as charged. The more the recipient(s) deny it, the more the establishment will use intimidating communicating tones, physical abuse and fake character name calling. If recipient(s) still denies accusation then 5. The establishment will use the Acts of Kindness done in number one as justification to be appalled by recipient(s) "fake" behavior then 6. Ends the abusive conversation with since you did this, you owe me for what I did for you; be it verbal encouragement, physical and financial deeds then 7. Abruptly leaves scene location. No matter what the recipient(s) says, does and or commits to in trying to keep the establishment from leaving, the establishment leaves anyways. All communication is blocked as though the establishment is never coming back again. Abandonment feelings, hypnotizes recipient(s) to become depressive, condemnation and feeling horrible for not being understanding grips the recipient(s) minds and hearts. Once cycles through a few times for days, the recipient(s) forgive establishment's behavior and tries to reach out in a desperate suicidal way of wanting to help the establishment fix/get beyond it's "behavioral" patterns; to enjoy a more enriching life with the recipient(s). Days perhaps months go by then 8. Establishment apologizes for its disrespectful behavior. Recipient(s) accepts and believes it's a break through in their relationship then 1. The establishment offers Acts of Kindness again to reassure the recipient(s) that it's a sincere apology; which is the beginning of a new cycle. Each cycle is a down ward spiral in the relationship with the recipient(s). The recipient(s) can not see it due to their belief that their relationship with the establishment is the best it gets, even if it means the death of them as a person; as an entity.

Simpler example: Establishment offers free privileges to recipient(s). Recipient(s) use them. Consider their selves privileged. Establishment takes an event and blows it out of portion. Recipient(s) responds to their best of abilities. Establishment blames the system for failing the recipient(s). Recipient(s) feel guilty for not contributing to privileges. Establishment makes intimidating threats to take away privileges, if certain criteria/demands are not met. Recipient(s) comply and or rebel. Establishment abandons recipient(s), to give them the feeling they lost the best thing that's ever happened to them. Recipient(s) get depressed, suffer lost and or rebel; more than likely suffer a set back, that makes them more vulnerable into being willing to except a "new better" privilege, from the establishment. Establishment appears to be sincerely apologizing to recipient(s) and offers a "new better" privilege to verbally make up for the previous loss; which it never fully follows through with. This is the start of a new cycle. If the recipient(s) can honestly look back over their relationship with the establishment, they would see how much more badly off they are, then what they was before. The recipient will have to decide to continue its depressive state and die. Or wean itself off from the establishment; slowly/wisely enough so that the establishment does not realize it, because of its self induce hypnotic addiction to self-centerism.

This is a form of religion. Religion is a group of routines accepted by its believers, as a form of human made salvation. This salvation is an empty void, which can never be filled, with a never ending list of dos and don'ts.

This can happen to any entity be it: religious, care providers, manufacturing, medicine, governments, etc…

Financial Bubbles

There are two types of financial bubbles; tangible and intangible.

Tangible Financial Bubbles (TFB or TFB's) are composed of supply and demand variables that can be visually detected by the general population. An example of a TFB comes from the commodity, product and banking industries.

Commodities: The value of the commodity can be felt and visually seen on an economic scale. The real value examples that I can feel in my wallet are; the cost of living, budgeting and savings.

Products: The value of the product can be felt and visually seen when we go to places of distribution, friends and quality. Places of distribution; how full are the shelves, sales, etc. Friends; depending the social economical status, how common is the product in their homes? Everyone has to have it or yesterday's old news? Quality; how well is it built?

Banking: The value of the product can be felt and visually seen when we go to our local bank to see how high or low the interest rate is. If it's low, people will have the tendency to borrow for more things. If it's high, people will have the tendency to save money as an investment.

Intangible Financial Bubbles (IFB or IFB's) are composed of variables that are unpredictable and uncountable both in monitoring the growth and rate of return of the bubble. An example of an IFB comes from the educational, service and governmental industries. Even though these contain products and services within their industry for the general population; the supply and demand variables can not be visually detected by the general population.

Educational: The value of getting a diploma and associates, bachelors, masters, doctorate degrees have no set value to justify the cost of obtaining one. Educational institutions are more interested in building their brand versus how successful the student will be based on skills learned. The kicker variable is after the degree is earned there's no guaranteed by the institution a minimum set salary will be earned per associated degree. It is up to the individual on how they apply their variety of required classes they trusted the institution to get their degree. Now the added twist to this kicker variable is professors. How well do they teach the subject? Are they able to custom teach each student to the needs of the student? Or insist the student just gets it. How well did they apply the subject to actual on job experience? Abstract? There are no set standards. Every teacher and professor has different opinions, goals and styles of teaching. Every student has different opinions, goals and styles of learning. Add exponentially to this problem is the local economy. If it's booming, then chances are good the education will pay for itself. But God forbid, if the economy is tanking, then the graduated student will need to move to another city, in hopes of recouping their investment.

Service: The value of the service is perceived by the user. If the user has a lot of extra cash, then paying higher than necessary costs are secondary to the user's concern in showing themselves in a "higher" social economic status. If the user is barely making ends meet, no matter how high the service cost are they will not purchase it. In that user's mind the higher than necessary cost has no value to them, period.

Government: The value of the service is currently undetermined by all the parties involved in obtaining the service and all those who are not obtaining the service. This type of bubble is the ultimate intangible financial bubble of all time and dwarfs all the other types of bubbles combined. What makes this the ultimate, is the Government is the only entity that can print its own money to operate. If that government thinks it can print an endless supply of money to cover all of its promised services then that government has lost control over its citizens, resources and security.

Macro Bubbles: Large scale entities that go pass State and National borders; including Christian denominations, alliances, ocean and air freight networks, defense and offense systems, geo-political, etc.

Micro Bubbles: Entities confined to one or more Cities within a State, Local Schools, Churches, Clubs, non-profits, co-ops, etc.

Prophecy: Bubbles Bursting

And the pops go boom. At first that didn't make sense. But thinking a tad deeper, it's like a sonic boom. The snap is heard then a deep thundering sound follows in sync. The same thing happens with these bubbles when they are ready to pop. Instead of the sounds of thunder being heard, we hear the cries of the masses being affected by their hope being destroyed in an instant, as their industries bubbles burst wide open. Fresh hot air of stories of hope keeps getting blown into the same old piece of gum, that's been chewed for weeks, until it finally pops.

Symptoms of an entity that is healthy and has a lot of life into it to go/live: the employees are consistently happy to be doing their job and not necessarily because of their wages and benefits are meeting their needs and some. Upper management is manually working with the "general" employees to create an open, positive and fluid environment and their customers can feel it. This theme facilitates and multiplies healthy and balance growth for the entity and its employees.

Symptoms of an entity infected with an establishment: A "we" and "they" mentality amongst hourly and salary employees. Favoritism is with workers who work less versus the good ethical workers. A justifiable calculated slipping away from going by the company hand book. Senior employees are subtly being harassed. Upper management and or owner(s) are seen rarely and or work two to three hr days and leave. Intimidation and condensing communication tones are common. Arrogant pride; A "we are too good for you" mentality. Those who can't afford their lifestyle and routines are considered "low life's." Main focus is on window dressing issues. It's what I wear and drive takes precedence over serving the employees by example with "it's an honor and privilege." Break down in inter department communication. Leaders giving work assignments to other department employees, without going to that department's leader. Taking authority away from the departmental leaders; who use to be making on site decisions. Quality is replaced by cheapening the integrity of the product and or service, without letting the clients/customers/citizens know about it. Forcing random policy rules on the good workers and not on the bad workers; creates animosity between workers, leaders and departments. Company justifies losing sales and or not growing new accounts.

A Media Entity infected with an establishment becomes habitually wired to give life to its agenda by spinning the most probable eye and ear captivating event's content, just to justify its unworthy existence. If you will, getting their fifteen minutes of fame. It justifies pointing their finger at the person who appears to be desperately choosing their short term fame versus taking the time to develop the Media's long term branding. Where all along, the infected Media's Entity was guilty of chosing to produce fifteen minutes of fame shows. Their focus is building a system that produces their continual source of programming fifteen minutes of fame moments, 24/7 for their network. *Think a little deeper on this.* The more viewers that Media entity can retain, the higher they can charge for their advertising venue. Now, wouldn't it stand to reason, that the Media Entity would focus on viewing content that Advertiser is advertising too, so that Media Entity could maintain that high income revenue stream; from that high paying Advertiser? Ok.

Another step deeper. What if that Advertiser Entity was infected by the same Establishment? Or at least one Entity was the parasite of the other Entity?

Establishment Routines: Establishment loves, thrives and insists everything associated with it follows a predictable pattern. The establishment chooses the best pattern to suit its hunger and incorporates it into its clients, customers and citizens. This pattern over time becomes more demanding. If left alone, it will come to a crescendo; this crescendo phase is when the bubble pops. A good example of this would be the life cycle of a black head pimple.

Dismantling an Establishment: The individual and or group of people, must have an independent network of resources; increase the chances of rooting out an Establishment, by disrupting the establishment's predictable feed pattern(s). Then at scheduled increments a new inverse routine must be persistently established, to the point of becoming self-perpetuating in disrupting the establishments incorporated routines. It's like introducing an antibody (penicillin) into an infected human body every six to eight to twelve hours a day for "x" days. To speed the process of dismantling an infect establishment, one must incorporate new multiple random inverse routines. More is better. The more controlled the better at tweaking the results.

When someone and or a group of people randomly inject new inverse routines into the establishment's network, it will cause the establishment to become chaotic and confused. Examples would be: cutting off the supply chain(s), ignoring intimidating rhetoric, etc… Support the means of supplying a cheap tangible cure and the infected medical industry will come undone, self implode and the lights are turned off permanently etc…

It's like cutting the loose threads on a garment. At first it appears that the problem has been fixed. Then to find out later it becomes a nice size hole in the garment; in this case, a hole in the bubble as it makes the noise POP!!!

Establishment Losing Control: As the desperation sets in, the establishment will have the tendency to take little "character faults" and escalate them into huge dramas, to scare/intimidate it's citizens clients customers, into believing that the establishment is right'; a how "dare you" question our judgment and goals tone.

This white knight that is coming to save the infected entity will be betrayed as an reckless imbecile, in hopes of deceiving their citizens, that mutiny of the establishment is foolishness and will be considered treason. In reality, this is proof that the establishment is evolving from portraying itself as innocent to intimiding styles of communication. This is a sure sign that the establishment lacks: self-confidence, the cognitive skills to adjust to independent flexible schedules and compassion.

If the establishment of the entity is convinced a "Donald Trump" person and or group of "Donald Trumps" are successfully dismantling the establishment, the establishment will relax and play dead; as though it is dead, in hopes of convincing the "Donald Trump(s)" into leaving the entity unguarded. So that it can re awaken and continue it's self-centered, suffocating cycles again, but more aggressively, in fear the "Donald Trump(s)" will return; with an undying desire to completely irradiate the establishment for once and for all.

Establishment in Melt Down Mode: It will change the rules daily, not remembering what it said previously and if brought to its attention, it will "spin" the proof away and or "make up" new reasons why the changes are necessary, while providing "fake" support for the change. If one would step back in the distance, they could see the establishment is in confusion. This confusion will cause the establishment to start attacking itself internally. Even though the establishment is propagating it's a trust worthy function, within the entity, it will not trust its loyal members. This will breed infighting and the final implosion of the establishment.

At the last few moments of the establishments life, it's creator(s) will come out of hiding and put in pleads for mercy requests, along with "I will serve you" tones and "together" we can obtain so much more than we can individually" classic cliché themes. All are self-centered lies.

A variety of people will be working for the establishment. There are two types of people who are good candidates for recycling pieces of the entity to build a whole new replacement entity. People who are unaware of the intent of the establishment and selfless people who out of compassion help the establishment to complete its goals; not knowing their being used. Once these types of people realize the true purpose of the establishment, they will do what they can to slow down and or dismantle as much of the establishment as they can as one person and or as a group.

Sober Reality: *If God does not intervene at the critical death moment of the entity by the establishment, the entity will die. If God has mercy and intervenes on behalf of the people, who are apart of the entity then the people will live to see the day; when the establishment will be removed from and or deceases controlling the entity. It doesn't have to be a person and or an organized group of vigilantes; it simply can be a natural disaster, a death, etc*

Donald Trump

Donald Name Definition: Someone who is strong in material matters, stubborn, great chief, kingly name, good business ability, good worker, steady, determined, practical, builds with responsibility well, a doer, down-to-earth, serious-minded, reliable, self-disciplined, good power of concentration, frank, methodical, believe in law, system and order.

The above qualities may bring a position of authority and power that allow you to create freedom and opportunities to enjoy life, to go places and to do adventurous things, willing to take risk to achieve your objectives, new ways and new experiences can't satisfy your restless nature, one accomplishment leads you to another, honesty and fairness guide your decisions knowing you will receive justice and honesty from other people in return, personal growth is vital...

Donald Trump Weak Points: are like a doctor cutting the cancer out of his patient but doesn't restore the wholeness of his patient; in regards to full and or better body health strength before the cancer drained the patient's life. There's the doctor who loves cutting/chemoing the cancer out of the patient repeatedly until the patient dies. Then there's the doctor who cuts the cancer out and cures the patient for the rest of the patient's life. So it is with these "Donald Trump" types. What good is it, if I window dress fixing a problem(s); with the appearance of balancing budgets, prosperity, etc, only for it to come back and bankrupt the system again?

This Donald Trump type person does not have to be religious and or the political status quo at the moment just naturally wired with a passion to recycle bankrupt, non-efficient and or out dated entities into a valued benefit to its clients/customers/citizens at or close to zero overhead. Note: Religious is referring to someone who routinely participates with like minded believers, minimum of one to three times a week. This committed routine assures fellow believers that routinely person must be a faithful believer. This routine allows leaders to use reference documents to use subtle intimidation, condemnation and control, with a list of dos and don'ts. Just because Religion believes in a God or gods doesn't mean its void of bubbles that go pop too. *2 Timothy 3:5 NIV. "Having a form of godliness but denying its power. Have nothing to do with such people." Luke 16:8 NIV "The master commended the dishonest manager because he had acted shrewdly. For the people of this world are more shrewd in dealing with their own kind than are the people of the light.*

Classic Greats with Weaknesses: King David had his adultery. Daniel Boone had his temptation of appearing to be disloyal and Joan of Ark her lack of stamina. Their weaknesses could have easily destroyed everything they had worked so hard to attain, for their countrymen and women. The King David's the Daniel Boones and the Joan of Arks are classic versions of a "Donald Trump" type person. These individuals were not perfect by any means. They lived and ate with the common people daily. They evenly split the spoils of war. They blended well with the everyday people because they were everyday people. They spoke, clothed themselves and bore their same pains. The only difference is God gave them the talent to network the people's skills into over throwing the tyrannies (the establishments) of their day. They would rather defend their dignity and honor versus saying sheepish sorries.

Being Presidential: What ever that means? More than likely this and or these "Donald Trump" type people will not be "Presidential" as pertaining to the type of Presidential everyone has come to know for over the last hundred plus years. Most recently it has pertained to being "politically correct and inspirational" in everything the President faces. Fancy words and humor can last so long then the people are looking for real change versus fake created change; with artificial but good sounding statistics, unaccountable spending and fake peace.

"Donald Trump" Phobia. Terminology for someone and or someone(s) having the fear that a "Donald Trump" type person(s) is/are going to make their situation(s) worse due to NOT knowing what the new outcome(s) will be. More than likely someone with "Trump" Phobia lacks the cognitive skills to adapt to the new changes; due to

21

a protected, well supported, self-centered lifestyle. When the establishment within the entity feels like it is losing control of bleeding to death the entity, it will go on a "Crucify Donald Trump" type person rampage. This over dramatization expresses to the general public, that there is really something wrong with the system and ends up promoting more of these "Donald Trump(s)" at the expense of the establishment versus at these "Donald Trumps" type people expense. The establishment would be better off acting like nothing is wrong and ignoring these "Donald Trump" type people. Example: When someone would ask, "What do you think of this "Donald Trump" type person? What are they're saying? Etc... Then the establishment infected media would respond back, "Who?", "Didn't give it much thought. Everyone has their option and soap box to say it from. They can do it on their time and dime, not ours." In other words, blow it off. Don't invite them; don't cover them, etc... Usually this occurs, in the front half of the establishment's infecting an entity. As it gets rooted, becomes the brain and heart of the entity; the establishment loses what little discretion and wisdom it had over to its addiction to being more self-centered in, with and through everything that makes up the entity.

Recycling Entities

When the establishment's bubble pops within the government system; this reality will snap it out of its hypnotic state. Those "Donald Trumps" that will be present, at that time this happens, will recycle the damaged pieces into the new USA 2.0.

The recycle transitioning smoothness with these entities will depend on the accuracy of the Auditing Efficiencies Teams. An Auditing Efficiencies Team will be comprised of successful business people who come from low overhead entities, reward their employees generously and or are employee own companies. Auditing these entities will be accepted by all people, except those who were dedicated to keep the establishment alive within the entity. Auditing will be the facilitator that speeds up the process in recycling infected entities. Once the positive results kick in and the masses begin to benefit from it, it will be easier to gain support in Auditing entities like Social Security, IRS, and Federal Reserve etc.

The following are some examples on how these government resources will be recycled.

The IRS Bubble: As in the Internal Revenue Service. Most people cringed when they hear those three letters. Their responses afterwards are the sound of the bubble popping. It implies that the government is in the business of taking money from people in various forms, with consequences if they do not comply. This is more of rule by intimidation versus I believe so much in this country that I want to make volunteer contributions to it. Flat tax is in and all the suggestions of retooling the tax structure is just another attempt of the establishment to sustain itself versus sincerely putting the citizens first. It will be terminated permanently. The left over resources will be converted into Automated Tax Collection System; on the implemented Federal Sales Taxes on products purchased. This will eliminate Federal Taxes on Income and no filing yearly taxes. This eliminates all deductions, intimidation, insider trading and favoritism.

SSI Bubble: As in Social Security Income. Most people are aware this has become an added benefit to the welfare system. Most any form of handicap will be entitled to receiving benefits. New definitions of being handicap are added as time goes on. Resources will be converted into the individual's self funded financial independent account and or 401(fi). All current paying into and retirees will stay on same system. Anyone entering the employment for the first time will be paying into these new 401(fi)'s. Withdraws will be tax free. In this shut down mode, SSI will be not accepting any new handicap applicants. Families of new handicap applicants will need to apply for assistance from other sources; like Foundations, MIRROR etc.

Department of Education Bubble: Outdated since the 1990's when the public school children would bring bombs to school and or make bomb threats to the school. Defiantly a serious jump up from "sit ins" of the 1960's 70's. Open gun firing on fellow students made things worse and caused a lot of parents to seek other forms of getting an education versus through the public school system. Another subtly that wouldn't make sense until around 2010's was the autism epidemic, that most public schools still don't get, unless there happens to be a teacher who personally lives with it. These three symptoms are sounds of the Public School Systems bubble about ready to burst. To hold this bubble in tact, the regulations keep pouring on the children's parents. The craziest is threatening the parent jail time if they do not comply in sending their child to their assigned school district. These are all the sounds of the Department of Education's Bubble Bursting.

There is no saving this system. An outdated system trying to get children; who play multi-button joy stick video games, non-stop for hours while avoiding multiple distractions, to stay focus on "winning" the game, to learning abstract answers to 1950's style of teaching. Oh, and let's add what Life Long Learning really is. It means being in debt for the rest of the students life without getting the job that will pay for its degree(s). Unless the student is willing to leave it's family rooted community, to another city and state to start building a new life from scratch. This only benefits the teachers and the professors who want a guaranteed income for life.

So this is how the Public School System will be saved. No teachers union. Teachers will be terminated if they can not assist the student in becoming skill at something. It's the same concept is when I get new tires for my truck. I expect the new tires, I just bought to perform as stated based on meeting a normal type of wear and tare, during the life of the tires. Now, if I found out they put retreads on my rims, and they prematurely blow off the rim going down the highway. I take my receipt and go back to the tire store and say. You put the wrong tires on. I get refund and never do business with that store again. I add to this by telling all my friends that tire store is fraudulent. Same applies to everything else in life.

The frame work is what drives the whole teaching system. The new frame work will be based on students graduating at 12 yrs old with all the basics mastered. Then the student does college until 16yrs old. Students graduate at 12 versus 18; then college at 16 versus 22. Now if the student wants a Masters they go another 2 yrs to make it 18 or PHD at 20. Keep the adult age at 18yrs old; drinking at 21 yrs old.

This will eliminate students dropping out at 16yrs of age and becoming a burden to themselves, communities and government.

The college phase will be teaching the student a skill that they can do with their hands; be it: carpentry, masonry, professional sports, doctoring, teaching, sales, administration, etc working with retired professionals in their communities.

The format on how the student will learn the basics will be done by the profession they choose in the beginning. So the student will have multiply ways of learning the same basic concepts and will contribute to building a solid foundation for their college years from 13 to 16 yrs of age. With virtual reality becoming an accepted form of communicating, all this basic schooling will be done in the convenience of the student's home during the convenient times of the student.

Extra curricular activities; sports, music, skill trades, etc will be done at the city's community center; perhaps an old public school house recycled into the city's community center, which is owned and operated by the city at zero land taxes, utilities exempted by the local energy company and maintained by the local lumber company and skills tradesman teachers mentoring the apprentice students on facility repairs and up keep of grounds. Everybody drives and or car pools their children/students to the community center. And the better version is, the Parents are actively working and participating with their curricular activity.

These formats will be the most efficient and closest to zero overhead while assisting the student/citizens in harnessing their personal passion in life. Once the individual learns how to prime their own well of their life's passion, nothing will stop them in their way of living their life to it's fullest potential. The life of being told to do something turns into the life of I need to do this next because this is what I love to do. No more need of teachers acting like baby sitters, playing testing head games and school systems threatening parents with fines and jail time.

SBA Bubble: As in Small Business Administration will be dismantled. The resources from the SBA and IRS will be recycled into the Mentoring Innovation Royalty Revenue Opportunity Resources. MIRROR for short. Resources will be recycled into assisting entrepreneurs in developing their concepts into viable businesses. If the idea seems doable, the idea will go through phases of proving itself marketable. If it passes each phase then continue support will be given until the idea is implemented in the market place. Once this specific idea goes live in the market place, the Federal Sales Tax that it earns from this specific idea will go into funding MIRROR. MIRROR will be self-funded at that point.

Jobs do not come from implementing business zones, offering tax break incentives and enforcing unnecessary regulations. Jobs are created from creative new products and services that are offered to their clients/customers/citizens at affordable prices while increasing their budgeting efficiencies and options of usage. Once the product and or service is accepted as necessary and viable then is that entity's responsibility to compete against itself in order to keep it's jobs for it's employees. Another words; creativity creates jobs, competition keeps them.

Global Warming Bubble: Global warming, everybody has a spin on it. Here's one that keeps me thinking hmmm. What if the earth is returning to its original pre Garden of Eden state of existence? There was no oceans; just streams/ rivers, geysers and artesian wells. It was like there was more water vapor in the skies to create a green house effect. The green house effect allowed life to live longer and healthier. Once this theory begins to show evidence the Global Warming Bubble will pop.

Defense Department Bubble: Defense and Offense Systems are only needed when there is lack on a planet. As each country harmonizes itself with the planet, there will be no need in the temptation of taking from others. As this manifests, this will be the sign the bubble is popping.

HUD Bubble: Dissolves into Independent Living Housing. The entity focuses only on: 1. Funding/backing dwellings structures that are self efficient. Stand alone off the "grid" type dwellings; powers itself, rain / atmospheric water containment systems. 2. Elderly, Vets and the handicapped (immobile): home repairs / purchases / in home living assistance modifications. Royalties from Patent Innovations for the different types housing needed for the different types of terrain (mountains /lakes /rivers /oceans /sky /space /other planets), old and new city layouts and weather conditions, will fund this entity.

Medicare and Medicaid Bubble: Will be dismantled and 100% replaced by Independent Health Care account's; owned by the individual. Funded by 5% of persons income. Withdraws tax free and only for health related issues. Once the fund reaches a minimum; like $250,000.00, anything above that amount is taxed

10% yearly. Automatically deducted by the Investment Company and deposited into a Handicap fund, that helps those people who are handicap and was drawing this income from the old SSI system.

VA Bubble: The word "veteran" general meaning refers to some one having experience in a particular field. This is too vague to describe the military personal and their service of potentially losing their lives while protecting their countries. This dissolves into Citizen Protection Services. As sobering as it sounds the local police, fire fighters, child and adult protection services and military need to emerge as one new response entity. Keep the color clothing to distinguish the division of service but wearing the pin will be "citizen protection." This will get rid of this subliminal bad taste of being the police of the world stigma. Any of the personal can transfer into any division and get years of service credit. Example: they serve outside the countries borders as patriots for other countries for four years, transfer to their local "police / fire fighter / community doctor / administration (major-president) / etc" for another 16 yrs or whenever (minimum 20 yrs) then retire from "active duty."

This will allow all the different independent types of service work together, understand the total concept of citizen protection. "Job" placement and hiring a "Vet" come a thing of the past due be absorbing into another form of service. If I currently volunteer to join military service then more than likely I will like that form of work. This new entity will give those who join to do Foreign Service will know automatically they will have a "job" related to domestic service.

Framework of promotion goes: I must serve in Foreign Service first before I can serve in domestic service. Both will build a respect for each other. No favoritism at the local level.

Note: Judges are separate 3rd party/neutral arbitrator's entity, which are all elected by the people; not appointed. Funding comes from the Federal Sales Tax.

Dept of Labor Bubble: Reabsorb under Citizen Protection Services as a division of. People have rights as a citizen, no matter what the role they choose to be, as a citizen of their country.

FDA Bubble. Food. Organic. Period. Dissolves into the Citizen Protection Services. Emphasis on converting 20th century scorching the land; with chemicals and GMOing plants and animals, back into natural created versus self-motivated manipulate versions, propagated for short term profits, with long term eco health problems.

NASA Bubble: Engulfs the Federal Air Traffic Controllers. Should be sending manned space vehicles together in case one malfunctions they have an immediate back up on hand. Distant explorer vehicles should doubled up as well; like land rovers, satellites, etc.

FBI/CIA/Secret Service: Combined to reduce redundancy. No other recycling. These will be the three agencies that will be able to boast of being apart of the original ebb and flow of the US Gov't over time.

Federal Reserve Bubble: Abolished. Go back to gold standard. Its not the gold that magically makes economies steadily grow, it's the accountability factor incorporated into the system of building wealth the old fashion way; by earning it with sweat, brawn and time versus inflating it artificially when a entity feels like. I can not spend outside my means. Everything will deflate proportionately. Medical costs will get in line to what the individual and families can afford, versus using fear to motive people to have unnecessary procedures and maintenance medications, taken without any guarantees of getting better and or cured. The same goes with other over inflated industries. Pay back Funds: Offer them as an On Going Tax Credit until all used up. Example: If bond was $10,000 give holder tax credit up to $10,000 plus interest that it was bought at, accrued over time of taking tax credit. Allow tax payer/business up to 7 yrs to redeem. If doesn't then automatically start refunding over a 3 to 7 yr period.

EPA Bubble: Current premise would be recycled into the *Toxic Chemical Conversion Agency.* It's not about controlling and isolating a list of toxic substances into approved waste containers, which generates a lot of addition waste of time in stock piling and managing that waste; that more than likely will waste other forms of natural life in and around the area; that the toxic waste is contained. Let alone, all of the other countries around the world, not doing anything to contain it. It's about creating tangible processes, which converts the toxic substances into new forms of natural eco products and or convert toxic waste back to its natural form. I know it's hard to convert plastic back into oil. But number one mandate then promote plastic being form into a organic biodegradable product; that is not toxic to the environment, by a certain date. Number two, what ever can be chemically converted into a product, can be chemically converted back. A process was discovered to chemically create a new product, so can the discovery of a process chemically covert the toxicity of toxic waste, back into its natural state of existence. Thus the eliminating the waste at it's end use versus creating unneeded waste management industries; that are adding unlimited burden to its clients, customers and citizens. The added benefit of converting toxic waste at it's source, allows for those areas of limited life forms restricted to limited resources, to continue to thrive versus an either or outcomes. Either protect the limited life form or produce this toxic waste and the limited life form dies. This breakthrough new technology will allow us to live and travel to other planets, due to being able to convert toxic substances into organic natural forms of substance; that naturally inter react with our bodies and life forms on planet earth.

Plus the other 600+ agencies:

The idea is to eliminate and consolidate all these agencies into about a half of dozen divisions to eliminate the redundancy in setting up the basic generic administration support staffs. Centralize the staff decentralize the authority to implement locally. Real time data polling with computers allows this to occur with working leadman on location versus a lot a double checking, from multiply layers of unnecessary management. It's like charging way more for a product or service and making tons of profit from it, only to hide that profit with tall luxurious buildings and over paid "upper management" so that corporate raiders won't engage in a hostile corporate take over for its high cash reserves.

Note: The names of the new recycle departments/agencies are suggested names only and may or may not be the final names of said entities.

The following are some examples on how other types of resources will be recycled.

Humane Society Bubble: Will be converted to WildLife Preservation Reservations. Expand wild life refuge zones that build wildlife eco cycle populations exponentially in arid (desert) type environments. Deserts and or desert conditions occupy one third of the earth's surface. Balancing these eco systems would create new habitable land for future larger human populations. As of the writing of this prophecy current estimated human population is 7 point something billion, with desert space a third of the earth's land surface. Convert desert space into habitable space, would allow human and animal life populations to expand to higher levels more comfortably, peacefully and efficiently. Royalties generated from any new technology created to these positive organic outcomes would fund this. Growth rate would mirror royalties earned rate. Energy harnessed from solar grids would fund as well. This end goal would be use these successful proto type technologies for creating habitable environments on inhabitable planets.

Science Bubbles: Enviably the deeper science can probe and "manipulate" "dna" the realization will be so "black" and "white" obvious, that Science WILL learn so much more, if it understood how things flow together already. Science as an entity, for the last few centuries has been infected with an establishment; known or unknown, that has to base its premise on; things are evolving chaotically and we can tweak the chaos by changing the quantities on a list of items and calling it science, knowledge and furthering the "life span" of human species. Blah. Blah. Blah. This is a premise that an establishment would incorporate through out the whole network. This type of premise would allow science to create charts of limitations, to possibly motivate fear, higher prices and artificially rationing resources.

What happens when an assumed truth is proven to be false? Like when the whole earth was perceived as being flat. Christopher Columbus proves it's not. It changes Ocean travel forever.

When the premise changes to, that everything is perfect and in harmony now, then scientist can focus in the mechanics of how everything flows together; down to the smallest details. The drive would be to harnessing natures natural balancing itself without chemically altering its molecular structure. Examples: Like the steam engine, water wheel. These are simple but harmonizing with nature.

Past and Current as of date of this published book, has been based on the premises of things evolve in the chaotic soup of life. Strong survives with no accountability. As technology and understanding goes deeper than the nano level; the premise will become, life is composed of three types. The balanced design of life is God the Father, The Manifestation of the balanced design of life is God the Son and The Liquid flow of the manifestation of the balance design of life is God the Holy Spirit. Note: It will be also commonly accepted that gas and liquids are the same. These two will be emerged into light and heavy liquids. Light liquids would be air and space; heavy liquids would be water to liquid mercury. Both types would be stated in percentages. Example air is 5% liquid and mercury is 95% liquid.

Traveling through space is perceived as in several years to light years. But what if, we can hitch a ride on the sun solar winds that travel at a million miles per hour? Now traveling to Mars is accomplished in 10.5 days. Setting up supply chain to feed the Mar's populations is doable until Mar's can develop its own eco system. Traveling back to earth against the million miles an hour seems impossible? Not if I'm a sail boater. I know how to zigzag against the winds, so traveling by sail makes more sense now. It might not be the same day length as going with the solar winds but still not in years, maybe twenty plus days?

Glow in animal's eyes is the animal's soul. Their eyeball must be designed so that when light flashes into it the retina dials in an aerated way; something like window blinds.

Life is not based; on chemical reactions and or inter reacting chemicals. It is the byproduct of sound waves. Sound waves affect everything down to the smallest form of life/substance.

Medical Industry Bubbles: It has become more of a legal drug pusher system designed to get repeat business versus curing the patient. Once the heart, diabetes, cancer and Alzheimer "diseases" become of the past. Then doctors will become real doctors. More like the other skill trades industries. If the car dealer just barely fixed the vehicles engines and we had to come back every month for the same temporary fix we would be infuriated. Doctors will end up leaving the trade in groves. Those who stay behind will look at old age as more of a weak blood and dehydration problem. Grey hair is the result of weak blood. Saggy skin is the result of decades of dehydration. Others will learn how to do personalize adult stem cell 3d printing and bionic parts. DNA alterations will be converting to learning how to live in outer space habitations.

Think of it as, it's easier to doctor a grape then it is a raisin. Is this too small of an example? It's easier to doctor a plum then it is a prune. The body is shrinking due to the environment dehydrating the body. It' not just lacking water but the body parts are forced to shrink when the body is dehydrated; the thickness of the skin, vision, internal organs, etc. If they shrink to far, they stop to function then the body cannibalizes itself to survive and or repair the damage.

Culture Divide Bubbles: As air travel is reduced to traveling anywhere on earth in 2 hours or less, inter cultural marriages will become the predominate norm. The establishments that have controlled marrying within ones culture is traditionally a requirement will become obsolete.

Marrying within Same Age Group Bubbles: As the Cultural Divides come crumbling down, so will marrying within same age groups. It's not currently accepted in most cultures now, but for a good time in history up until the 1900's, there had to be at least fifteen years apart from the woman and the man. Example an 18 yr old woman would be able to marry a minimum 33 yr old man. It's not the woman is marrying a "daddy" figure; it's that the man will more than be established. He will have focused on getting established in his career, have a home and be more matured in dealing with providing, sheltering and having a family with a woman at that age versus mind frame of an 18yr old.

Language Barrier Bubbles: As Interpretating multiple different languages instantaneously becomes the predominate way of life, then need for printing and speaking different languages will become a thing of the past. Those establishments that are trying to slow this down to protect their profits will burst and become a thing of the past as well. Remember the Tower of Babel wasn't a bad thing. God was admiring their unity in accomplishing such a feat.… He confused their language so that we would realize we need Him to get to Him versus through our selfishness. Genesis 11:4 Paraphrased NFB. Would it be ironic that He confused our languages to challenge us to think deeper for one another, enriching, and when we put others first and go to build the next Tower of Babel 2.0; we will travel to multi-dimensions of the universe versus just one dimension.

Country *Barriers Bubbles:* As air travel anywhere on the earth becomes two hours or less, country barriers become obsolete. No need to hold people within a nationalized country.

Lawyers/Attorneys Bubbles: As artificial intelligence becomes a working tool, there will be no need for lawyers. The establishments that are creating more laws to protect and to deepen control of their industry, will disintegrate within a twinkling of an eye. Facts will be filtered to actual laws, which protect a person's rights of freedom, liberty and justices for all. The outcomes will be executed instantaneously, accurately and within the person's means.

The lawyers disappear but the jury remains. Each can defend themselves in the court of law versus articulations of manipulating loop holes in the judicial system; because most people are ignorant of all the recorded laws and the previous cases tried against the laws, to interpret the laws. Vigilantes become a thing of the past.

Retirement from Work Life Bubble: As human life means living longer to the 120 – 160yrs of age predominately common throughout all cultures, all living habitats; the Retirement Industry and Communities will self-implode. People will rethink on how they want to live their lives. Here are a few examples of what will happen. People will wait to have children, perhaps to their early 40's; having children farther apart to enjoy each child more personally in their toddler to teen years. And or having more children from the current 1 to 3 children to 5 to 9 children. Having multiple careers will be the norm; from the current 1 to 2 careers to 4 to 6 careers. With a percentage coming out of each check automatically going towards their Financial Independence Accounts by the time they get to their 5 or 6 careers, they will have plenty invested, based on a smaller amounts over time verses cram a chunk of the paycheck in for over a period of 20 to 30+ yrs versus 100 to 120 yrs. The compounding investment will be staggering versus "I hope the Markets don't tank out when I retire" thoughts will be a thing of the past. Now people can think more of how much space do I want to occupy. When schooling becomes independent of location, I won't be tied down to a school district for my child/ren. And travel gets less than 2 hours anywhere on earth, my location/s of habitat becomes more flexible, which in turn gives me more options with the different careers I want to be apart of.

Types of Careers Bubbles: Working for one company over a short life span becomes a thing of the past. I can either stay in one field or start fresh in different fields. Example of Career cycles will be maximum 20yrs; the cycle closes out. If I do well with my Financial Independent Account then I can start drawing out maximum one fifth of its value for big purchase items. Five career examples would be: 1st career would be in Service, 2nd career in Manufacturing, 3rd career in Sales, 4th career in Teaching and 5th career in Consulting.

Population Control Bubbles: Is purely an entity infected with an establishment control issue. It's fixated on controlling how the population inner reacts with each other while in its presence more than profits. To make up for lost profits it will artificially create a shortage so that the remaining population will be willing to pay more for their basic needs. During the establishment hiding within the entity phase, it initiates subtle forms of population control; mineral deficiencies, higher costs of living, divorce, etc.

Routine Bubbles: Routines are double edged swords. When I go from routine A to routine B and there is a positive change, I make the mistake of thinking that A is not as good as B. It's not that B is better; it's changing the routine that caused my senses to tune in on new resources and options. The new resources and options were always there. I had done routine A for so long it hypnotized me into having tunnel vision. The tunnel vision filtered out from seeing the "new" resources. I forget that changing the routine open my eyes to another solution and start worshipping the routine, as the thing that cure my problem; wince not. The starting of worshipping the routine is the sign an establishment has infected the routine. The sub conscious establishment will always be getting me to bow down to it; with artificial problems labeled as "see this is why you keep the routine" The signs of routines bubbles about ready to burst are; burn out, being depressed, not happy, weight gain or loss, lower tension spans, feel like life is going nowhere, boredom, rebellion, tired, etc.

Human No Value Bubbles: When societies are infected with an establishment, they justify throwing their own kind under the bus of no value. Be it children, women, elderly, race, culture, religion, etc. For children it would manifests as aborting children, pushing them through school and ending up with no tangible skills to earn an income, pumping them full of chemicals... women it would manifests as a various types of properties, etc... elderly manifests as reasons to isolate; to an assisted living facility, so that the next generation can seize their assets before their times, etc.... race, culture and religion manifests as hate crimes, etc

Autism Miss Diagnosis Bubble: Autism awareness is gaining the momentum it should have had 10 yrs ago, but the infected establishment held its ground all too well. These children/people are thinking multiple things at the same time; very clearly in their minds; and have a hard time focusing on "one" thing. It doesn't make sense to them when they can think of many things at once. A good comparison is Autistic people think of the whole word "people" and all the combinations related to it, whereas the non-autistic people are focusing on only one of those letters at a time, like "o" in the word people. To the autistic people they don't understand why they would want to focus on just the letter "o" when focusing on all the letters at once is more enjoyable. Once this connection has been accepted, translators will help the current general public understand/ interpret for people both types of thinkers. Point is, once the establishment has been removed, the world will be over inundated with tsunami waves of millions upon millions of super geniuses.

Terrorist Bubbles: When the terrorist entity accomplishes its goal and or not accomplishing it fast enough for its followers, the entity's bubble will burst. To "hold" the entity together; to keep the bubble from bursting, it will have to become more abusive with its followers. Its "code of honor" is meant to control its followers, with the least amount of abuse. The major sign of the bubble about to burst is when the terrorist entity starts killing its own; based on a paranoia there are spies within their entity.

Propaganda and Conspiracy Bubbles: Get their life from faulted ideologies, created by self-centered people, with no cognitive mental depth perception. These bubbles have various sizes. Examples: Entities needing to push bad and or over priced products and services to their consumers. Creating the stigma, that the entity has a high quality product; so therefore it is worth paying the high price for it, in reality it's just another product. Creating false shortages, etc. To larger bubbles that lead clients / customers / citizens into to believing "something" is needed for the greater good of everyone involved. As time goes on, the majority becomes convinced that it's not for their good. The majority minimizes their involvement as much as their means allow them. The bubble bursts.

Fade Bubbles: The next "new" things are created out of the general public, being tired of seeing and hearing the same thing over and over. The entity sensitive to this, will create an evolved acceptable contrast to what currently is in vogue. Simple example: Pants with medium flair bottoms that cover the top half of the shoe, to straight leg pants, that show the entire shoe and or boot. Cell phones that can't take photos to cell phones that can take videos. Some entities understand this so well, they have the "ultimate" end patented product upfront, but start out with a basic version of it. Over a period of time, several years, add "new" features to it to entice current owners to buy the "new" upgraded version. This would be an example of a control bubble bursting within the larger bubble that will burst eventually.

Movement Bubbles: Commendable causes more than likely create a following, which are sincerely trying to "help" a group of victims. As long as there is no fraud involved the cause grows and the victims can move on in the direction of hopefully a better life. The sign the entity is infected with an establishment is when stories of fraud occur; within its top ranking leaders. When the damaged has been done, the bubble has burst. The followers stop rallying around each other, become less loyal and move on. These include religious movements as well; revivals, resourceful religious leaders, etc.

Mineral Deficient Bubbles: Based on ignorance and or deliberately inflected to cause mass populations to search for "cures" due to their under nourishment. Once the cure is found on a mass basis, the bubble bursts. Simple examples of this are organic foods versus processed food. Processed food was more efficient to produce at a greater profit but ends up having very little nutritional value to the consumers. Higher level of sickness occurs, etc. Certain minerals might be present in the food but it's not in its eco bio state of existence. For examples; do online searches for the benefits of raisins, iodine, chlorophyll, bee venom, etc. As of publish date of this book these are mass mineral vitamin deficiencies through out the earth. Also look at what happens to fruit bearing trees when they have the minerals they need to exist and bear fruit. When there are ample minerals, no pesticides are needed to keep their predator pest at bay; the same goes for animals and humans.

Lemons balanced the body pH levels; anti-bacterial and increases the body's ability to absorb other minerals and vitamins.

Life of the food is from the energy it emits versus the food content itself. The high or low energy the food emits when consuming it, determines how much energy I have in doing things. Do online search for the benefits of bio wave generators curing all diseases.

Population Bubbles: Populations expand based on in the past, on the strength of a nation. With hi-tech defense and offense innovations, the need for "many" people needed to win a war has been curbed. It's not how many people a nation has now; it's whose weaponry is the most sophisticated. *The new minor reason* to have many children will be, the centralized mega cities will become historical museums of the 20th century and the populations will decentralize to rest of the earth's land and ocean masses yet not habituated; as of the date of this publication. Desserts will bloom, oceans and great lakes will populate, the untouched natural wonders of the earth, mountains and the skies. *The new major reason* to have many children will be to populate the solar system to utilize specific "new" resources for the greater good of creation; maximize the fullness of creation. (No reference to chemically engineering, even though it will be attempted

43

and capitalized on). Current family sizes are 1 to 3 children. Current small percentage of the families have 4 to 5 children. Where as when expanding throughout rest of the earth, solar and galaxy systems, normal family sizes will be from 5 to 9 children. Some families will have 12 to 18 children. When people live 240 or more years old, it will be common to see companions having multiple sets of families spread through out their lives. Example: the couple will have 5 to 9 children; enjoy that cycle of their children having children then fifty years later have another set of 5 to 9 children.

Population Habitat Bubbles: As habitat technology support systems become more harmonized with creation, the concept of huddling in largely populated cities will burst. The concept of the small farm 10 to 20 acre communities will explode.

Season Activity Bubbles: Major sports, at the time of publishing this book, play a major role in how people, families and communities interact with each other through out a particular season. When these major sport bubbles burst, they will affect how people interact with each other throughout the season. Odds are high that new major sports will be introduced, to offer a wider variety of interest to the people, who are not involved with the sports world. Sports bring families together; dissipate stress and the fundamentals of working as a team. The introduction of another major sport will burst the bubbles of the major sport entities; salaries, bonuses, benefits, etc.

Five Senses Bubbles: Sight, Hearing, Touch, Taste and Smell, etc. The individual five senses now become one mega sense. A glimpse at this would be looking through clear glass. If I look through the clear glass I see what's on the other side of the glass. If I look at the reflection on the glass I see another view. If I combine the two, I get a third view. This 3rd view is a pinhole glimpse at all 5 senses working together at the same time.

As nano technology creates useable wearable appliances that heighten our awareness, so will the clarity of our senses unite our subconscious with our conscious and our souls as one entity. Examples of wearable appliances are jewelry, clothing, etc. These will burst the bubbles of "tunnel vision," "I have to see it before I believe," etc. Those who can't visualize concepts will be able to literally see them now. Wearing glasses on my nose to basically view items clearly will be harnessing my "third" eye; to see items clearly in my mind fluidly versus on and off as I take my glasses on and off. Now let's upgrade all this basic info to being able to "seeing my hearing, touch, taste and smell," "hearing my sight, touch, taste and smell," "touching my sight, hearing, taste and smell," "tasting my sight, hearing, touch and smell," and "smelling my sight, hearing, touch and taste." Yah, blows my mind too when I first saw this!

Stereotype Bubbles: Applies as well to everything besides humans; it applies to establishments, parasites and foods. Supremacy groups are stereotype as whites only with full body clothing to hide their identities. Supremacy can infect anyone, any race and any creed. Current non-stereotype is ISIS, primarily Non-Caucasian and wear full body black clothing. Different types of mob organizations, etc. Parasites tend to be stereotyped as blood suckers, tape worms and or venom inducers. Plus, unseen fungi, scavenger bacteria and self-centered attitudes can be parasites as well. Food: raisins are seen as trimmings to any food group meal, where in reality it should be a daily critical nutritional foundation to the human body, if one is interested in long term health and longevity. And the lemon is stereotype as a pucker, preservative and weight loser. Where in reality it turbo charges the health and longevity provided by the raisins; along with balancing the pH of the human body, quieting the tempest of a flu, etc.

Various Sensation Bubbles: Be it drugs, sex, depression, obesity, drunkenness, immaturity, plus all the other forms of self-centerism will be replaced by the person's life passion.

Time Frame Bubbles: Currently on earth, we're biologically programmed to believing a day is twenty-four hours long. When planetary travel becomes the norm, this bubble will burst too. Age dating will start as I'm 55 years old on earth and I'm 29.7 years old on Mars. Then bounce to age of my body based on how dehydrated it is. To galaxy age then as traveling to galaxy to galaxy is within a few days then a Universe age will become more the norm. But the overall predominate age reference will be based my body's biological clock, when technology goes deeper than the nano level.

Emerging Bubble: These are bubbles that are currently growing but will burst later after technology gets more refined.

Bubbles Bursting Inside Bigger Bubbles: Simple example to describe this is the general stock market. Let's say the market has broken a new record but the economy is slipping into a serious recession, but everyone isn't bought into it – yet. The insiders know it, so they engage into a deep sell off. This is a bubble that has just burst within the bigger bubble. The market moves back up because the general public takes it as a good buying opportunity to buy more. As the market gets closer to its high; more news comes out that the economy is collapsing. A bigger sell off occurs; usually steep enough that everyone believes their in the middle of a recession. Panic selling takes place. No one wants to buy back in for awhile, due to the severe losses they incurred. This is a sign the big bubble has burst as well. This general logic can be applied to all entities.

Donald Trumps

Expect to see five different types of "Donald Trumps." These five types are: administrative, sales, teacher, care giver and visionist. These five different types are not necessarily five different presidents but more like the five different types that will be functioning together; in recycling the various different types of bankrupt entities sampled throughout this book.

The Administrative Type: This "Donald Trump" type successfully balances being accountable with marketing, training, care giver and aligning/networking them all together, to accomplish a goal and or goals that everyone can see clearly and how to obtain it; efficiently, effectively and under budget at minimal operating cost. They can successfully convert marketing product(s) and or service(s) into actual orders with clients/customers/citizens; that is greater than what the manufacturing entity can produce. The drive and appearance will be balancing functions with more of bottom line approach with time, resources and money.

This "Donald Type" would be more of what's good for everybody, no matter what the tax bracket, social economic status and or culture. This type is wired to keep in balance the new version of the entity throughout entire entity's life span.

The Teacher Type: This "Donald Trump" type likes to give working examples to students so they can better grasp on understanding concepts. They successfully assist the individual(s) into unlocking and priming the wells of their life's passion(s) into actual revenue, which provides for their basic needs and desired goals. They meticulously describe the details of the functions, what the functions can and can not do and when best to use them. A good teacher will give countless different examples in explaining the same thing, regardless of the student's attention span. They focuses more on making sure the concept is learned in its different applications versus on how it fits in the grand plan of the individual's life.

This "Donald Trump" type would love to work in a more of "blighted inner city project", etc. This type is wired to duplicate the new version of the entity throughout entire entity's life span.

The Care Giver Type: This "Donald Trump" type will go through the same pain of limitations to show compassion when assisting. Creates physical tangible senses of security while getting people to believe in themselves, that they can still obtain what they are unselfishly trying to attain. Successfully assists the individual(s) in meeting the individual(s) basic needs and desired goals, without compromising the individual's dignity. Be it emotional, companionship, shelter, mobility, financial independence, etc. The care giver gives without conditions, knowing their friendship and the individual will be better off, in the future from it.

This "Donald Type" would be more of a Francis of Cecily. Wired to sustain and nourish entity.

The Engineering Type: This "Donald Trump" type would be more a young Daniel taken to Babylon. He's quiet. Non-confrontational, a do it yourselfer and improves the quality of life for others and themselves, with very little effort. They appear to be laid back due to understanding the big picture and anticipating changes in current situations, which are evolving into their future state of existence, when others more than likely can not.

They are obsessed in building new solutions to solve current problems. No workable prototypes upfront. They mention a lot of abstract information that tends to come out confusing and not feasible. Once the prototype can be seen and easy to do, most of the general population embraces it as the new norm solution. They successfully articulate and implement hands on tangible efficient, effective, within budget proto-types, so that the other major types can visualize the "bigger picture/vision" from the working proto-type; to the point of physically implementing it into existence, with the group and within budget.

This "Donald Trump" type would be more of a Leonardo De Vinci. Loner type, inventor, sports buff, artist, etc... Wired to envision the mechanics of upgraded application of the entity and or new entity, designs it, proto types it and implements it.

Note 1: The type characteristic is apart of their daily life.

Note 2: The success rate for any of these types are determine by how well the person can connect all of the individual's life passions into the network and or on the team while keeping cost under budget.

Prescription: USA 2.0™

The election of a "Donald Trump" for a one man cure all is long term unrealistic. The gutting of government agencies for quick balancing of the budget will lead to vacuums within society, which more than likely will become the prey of the next election. Perhaps the fix will last for 20 yrs, then will there be another "Donald Trump" emerge to cure it all again? This seems to be more of making the status quo happy until their not, then reboot and start the cycle again with another "Donald Trump" leading the way. This prescription is more like politics as usual and how modern medicine treats its patients with monthly maintenance drugs, which their patients take for the rest of their lives versus permanently curing them. This too is a bubble that will be bursting sooner than later.

I see more of a permanent fix. One of which the founding fathers believed that the future US citizens would clarify restraint onto those who would find the loop holes in the constitution and exploit them.

First we will need to be selfless at heart and lifestyle to be able to find these solutions; then to maximize the efficiency of the solution with zero overhead. Once the proto type is proven to work then sustain it with self-sustaining resources.

Consumers control the market not the overhead of the entity. The strength of the market is at the mercy of the consumer.

It appears the founding fathers of the USA had no clue to what the US would be like in 250 years, while welding the constitution. Smart Phones, Internet of Things (Conception form of Artificial Intelligence) and Global Tracking are clueless concepts, let alone the daunting impact they would have on entities that use them. Regardless of how each of them saw the future, they more than likely shared the same view, that if her future citizens stayed to the constitution, they would have better light as to know how to strengthen the constitution; to prevent the establishment from using these new tools to worm their way into the government, to change it's behavior into a tyranny regime.

Even if it will take a "Donald Trump" type person or group of people to recycle the collateral damage the establishment causes, the current system doesn't protect itself from a fake type of "Donald Trump" from running in the future and be mistakenly elected based solely on the perception of the previous good results of the true "Donald Trump" accomplished in the past. To prevent the establishment from gaining complete control of an entity it must be surgically removed by the following accountability filter system.

This grid of prior presidential qualifications applies to the Future US Government. Before one can apply/run for the office of the President of the United States they must complete the following requirements to qualify:

1. Serve as Mayor of a City for 4 yrs.
2. Serve as a Congressman for 4 yrs.
3. Serve as a Senator for 4 yrs.
4. Serve as a Governor for 4 yrs.

5. Serve as a Vice President for 4 yrs.
6. If Elected as President Serve for 4 hrs.

*No Governing Leader can serve more
than 4 yrs per type of office.*

The following transitioning requirements will be needed to filter out the known and or unknown establishment leaders within the governing entity.

Currently anyone serving as a governing leader and has been for more than 4 yrs to date, that governing rep will be terminated at the next scheduled election; for that position and will be eligible to run for the preceding position if have not filled that requirement yet. If they have then they can move onto the next available position by election. Example if a senator has more than 4 years; his term terminates at next election date. If that senator has not yet been a mayor and or congressman, they are eligible to run for mayor position before congressman.

These positions of governing leader do not have to be filled consecutively year after year. That leader can take breaks in between positions. Example: Leader runs for mayor, wins, serves for 4 yrs. Term is terminated. Waits 8 years then runs for congressman, wins serves for 4 yrs. Term is terminated. Waits 4 yrs then runs for senator, ect.

All positions of leadership and decision making are elected by the people; there are no appointments. The following positions that were appointed will be terminated. The following positions will convert from appointment, to being elected by the people, for the people. Examples as follows: Agency heads, speakers of the house and senate, secretary of state, vice-president, supreme court justices, etc.

In regards to the office of the Vice-President; this office will now be the leader over 5 adjacent local states. Example: 50 states will create 10 vice-president positions. From these 10 Vice-president leaders the President of the US will be elected. No leader can serve for more than 4 years. After 4 yrs that leader can no longer serve in that position, any where in the US government; at local, domestic and foreign related positions.

Once a leader completes their full cycle of leadership positions, that leader can no longer serve the US Government. Period. They will only be able to serve as leaders in the non-profit and or corporate positions when avails.

This transition will take approximately six complete elections to cleanse the establishment from the US governing entity.

What is a Good Governing Leader? It's not a role that is reduced to outward appearances, both in clothes and colorful conversations – that's fantasy land. So the vulnerability is electing people, who have more than enough and have become foreigners within their own land, to the hardships of the rest of the citizens currently suffering from; poses of the "fat and living large" life. No matter how much they research the need; they will never understand the need, until they personally suffer the need and its daily challenges through out its entire cycle.

Rather a Good Governing Leader would be better chosen, if it were based on "it's an honor and privilege" to be a governing leader of United States of American and or any other country.

The people at the top of leadership responsibilities in governmental entities should not get paid. This will filter out the career complacent people who want it as a personal job versus operating the government entity for the purpose it was designed.

Selfless

If anyone believes there's a God, they will more than likely believe, God put this country together for not only His Purpose and Glory, but for people torn asunder in foreign lands; could come to her and find rest in her, in hopes of rebuilding their lives again.

"Give me your tired, your poor,
Your huddled masses yearning to breathe free,
The wretched refuse of your teeming shore.
Send these, the homeless, tempest-tossed to me,
I lift my lamp beside the golden door!"

This quote comes from
Emma Lazarus' sonnet,
New Colossus…

To expound on this would be best said
from the New Friendship Bible the
meditations reference…

'Come, you who are blessed by my Father; take your inheritance, the kingdom prepared for you since the creation of the world. For I was hungry and you gave me something to eat, I was thirsty and you gave me something to drink, I was a stranger and you invited me in, I needed clothes and you clothed me, I was sick and you looked after me, I was in prison and you came to visit me.'
Matt 25:34b-36

the tangible self application meditations in reference to the above reference…

Imagine God through my life's passion, feeding people's hunger for their life's passion.

Imagine God through my life's passion, quenching people's thirst for their life's passion.

Imagine God through my life's passion, inviting other peoples life's passions, to share in my life's passion.

Imagine God through my life's passion, clothing peoples life's passions, to cover up their vulnerability.

Imagine God through my life's passion, providing resources to people's life passions, to strengthen them.

Imagine God through my life's passion, setting people's life passions free from their barriers.

… New Friendship Bible
Meditations

Zero Overhead

With the current and near future computer technology, there is no need for upper management, CEO's and C whatever's. The 20th century entities milked this one to the bone. Luxurious skyscrapers filled with paper workers, multi-million dollar salaries, unbridled R&D departments and over-kill advertising campaigns; to absorb ungodly amounts of profit margins, that would been better off in the pocket books of their consumers. It's not how big my profit margins can get; it's how many consumers we can sell to. Mass volume with multiple options to Many Cultures is the driver. Creativity creates job; competition keeps them.

Why Zero Overhead: It's like building up immunity to establishments trying to infect it. Establishments are lazy. Their only desire is to take from those who are doing the hard work in making products and services with a value and or benefit, for a profit. The larger the profit margin, the higher the rate the entity will be infected with an establishment.

Ok. So we get to see the day where there is working supervisors, team captains if you will, that will have access to upper management information on computers making manufacturing and servicing decisions. Aah, sounds refreshing. This might sound like I'm union and hate upper management. Nah. Believe it or not, I've had at least 30 yrs of shipping and receiving manufacturing management and 7 yrs prior of, hourly break records machine operator experience. The biggest factor in slowing me down, was upper managements slow response times to decision. Obvious easy and minimum expense solutions took months to decide. And if there was any pride involved, shop floor ideas were twisted a tad so that upper management would declare it was their own idea. I loved working with the employees on the floor and interaction was easy, because I came from the floor. My office peers resented it.

This will work so long and fall apart like anything else that starts out with good intentions. The kicker to locking this all in and keeping the entities overhead close to and or at zero overhead, will be converting the entity to employee owned entities. This will be one of the 21st century's staples; employee owned entities will be the norm and a must to survive the long haul. This will make more common sense across the board with all walks of life, when the life expectancy of a human goes from around 80 yrs old to 160 to 240 yrs old. *Why employee owned entities?* They know more about the entity then anyone else within the entity. Supervisors are mediators, facilitators and baby sitters between hourly employees and upper management. They were the "first computers" of the entity. Upper management analyzes paper work statistics, public relations and absorbs large amounts of profits with high paying salaries. So with the computers replacing supervision and upper management, there will be a gap in accountability for holding quality standards, competivability and meeting supply and demand requirements. This gap is easily taken care of by employees who own the company. The motive of ownership creates the desire within the employees to excel in the entity succeeding so that they will succeed. Thus next to and or zero overhead is doable and easy to obtained. Desirable ratio of ownership between the person(s) who created and financed the entity to employees should be 30% owner(s) to 70% employees. This way the employees will always feel they control their destiny of the entity and the owner will stay connected with the company to maintain their envisioned goals/purposes, versus getting abandoning by inherited 2nd and 3rd generation children. These following generations get less and less involved, due to they were not the ones, who put their sweet and blood into the creation of the entity itself. The 2nd and proceeding generations are more likely tempted then the 1st generation, in allowing an establishment to infect the entity, in hopes of partaking from its short term profits vs sacrificing the sweet and blood like the 1st generation.

Self-Sustaining

If an entity can self-sustain itself then that entity can be self-perpetuating.

These are the changes that will take place to create the foundation, which takes the USA 2.0 through the rest of the 21st Century and into the 22nd Century; perhaps beyond.

The United States of American has shed the blood of her sons and daughters; so that other nations can be set free from their tyrannist regimes, more than any other nation since the beginning of time. To personalize the deeper impact of this, these sons and daughters gave up their legacies, so others can live theirs. No other nation on the earth has propagated the story and message of Jesus Christ to more nations, than that of the United States of America. These two core drivers from her heart alone; has set the United States of America up, to producing abundant future fruit, which will bless her future citizens and the world to enjoy, for centuries to come. It makes more since when I think about how she was birthed into existence, by personally setting herself free from her tyrannist that was border line suffocating her, with heavy taxes and regulations. This personal experience has become the DNA of her soul. When we see her stop setting other nations free momentarily, it will be because of an establishment infecting her, until she's hypnotized into believing, it's not her job anymore. It was never a "job" to her, it was and is her passion to prove to the nations; that when the people rule a nation, it will be that nations greatest moments in history.

Man is to serve each other vs one man serving the other man.

Epic Prophecy

Ok. Let's take a breather. We covered a huge pile of thoughts in a lot of areas, within 100 pages. Where does this all fit in the grand scheme of life. Ok, let's include the whole universe too! Nope, we've went over the edge in this book, so let's include all the people in the universe.

Ready? Let's go. For starters forget all the stuff they taught in history on the pre-industrial age, industrial age and post industrial age, then the service industry. Yes. This is all tunnel vision, with a limited view point that has been cast in stone as "this is it." **It's not.** This same logic is being use to institutionalize "global warming." Please "global warming" people, at least quote a scripture reference to better put this in a bigger picture perspective. The new earth will have no oceans, it will be restored to its original green house canopy atmosphere, after the firmaments above and below the earth have melted. Aka ice, made the oceans and the perfect time and place, to call it an "ice age." Ok. Sorry rabbit trails way off course. Sort of, it's the same logic.

Ok. Enough of all that stuff, let's talk juicy future revelations/prophecy that I can sink my investment portfolio teeth into and profit from it over this whole process time.

There are 3 Industrial Revolutions. The first is the Mechanical Industrial Revolution, the second is the Hologram Industrial Revolution and the third is Exponential Industrial Revolution.

Mechanical Industrial Revolution: This is the First Industrial Revolution. During the Mechanical Industrial Revolution; mechanical machines were created; from steam engines to driving by remote control vehicles on and by other planets. We are currently coming to the end of the first Industrial Revolution.

There is no such thing as the Service Industry following a post industrial era. Yep. I said it. There was never, is never and will never be a Service Industry Society. Service Industry has, is and will always be assisting to the needs of workers who produce a product or service for others to use. The service industry provides for the needs of the workers; day care, medicine, education, entertainment, etc. If a country is convinced it is a Service Only economy, then it is more than likely infected with an establishment.

Back to the First Industrial Revolution. During this type of revolution the mechanical machines started out simple (complex at the time of manifestation) such as a steam engine to now an actually complexed sensory activated computer system, that creates a beneficial result (commonly referred to as technology – it's still mechanical in nature).

People not able to see in the future the other two industrial revolutions, mistakenly say the current new technologies are service industry related, but in reality are the components that will be used in the Second Industrial Revolution. And the same for the Second Industrial Revolution will have the components that will be used in the Third Industrial Revolution.

Ok. Are you ready to absorb more? I am.

Hologram Industrial Revolution: This is the Second Industrial Revolution. This revolution will produce hologram machines, as with the first industrial revolution, will start simple. We are beginning to see some of evidence manifest in imaging devises, that allow us to see/envision things easier; which allows solving problems better and easier. This is the beginning point of the 2nd Industrial Revolution and the ending point of the 1st Industrial Revolution. Virtual Reality is a product of the Mechanical Industrial Revolution that allows its customers/clients/citizens to get a glimpse at how the Hologram Industrial Revolution will affect their world/habitat.

The Hologram Industrial Revolution will start out producing simple working useable devices that will work independent of mechanical devices. Towards the end of the Hologram Industrial Revolution the devices will be complex and operate like and or as the souls to the mechanical devices. A cliché example of this would be from the old sci-fi movies portraying people as androids.

Creating a Hologram into a likeness of a soul will be breath taking. The hologram will have internal sensors that will bring the mechanical device to "life" per say. The hologram soul will be able to detach itself from the mechanical device when key sensors have been severed. The hologram soul will have life of its own and appear as a ghost like figure with the first models. As progress it will be able to cloth itself and choose its desired form. Note: This all seems plausible and something from an "end day prophecy", only if one buys into the belief that either Christ will Rapture His followers before, middle of and or at the end of the "7 Year Tribulation Period." But with today's technology levels, it's going to be quite a while before this happens.

Most current observers of biblical prophecies believe it's going to be any day. It could be, but probabilities are high that it won't happen for what we currently consider a long time.

Hologram Soul^{TM} version machines do not have what is traditionally known as a centralized brain and heart. The brain and heart is through out the whole hologram entity. Even though it can be independent, appear to create a physical body (it's an allusion) and network with other Holograms to infect a whole galaxy; it is still independent. Its self-centerism limits its ability to gain control of everything. To enjoy its maximum life it must operate in unity with all other life. The more unity the more life it has.

Note: If the entities that use these devices are infected with an establishment, the entity will end up appearing as apocalyptic in nature.

If an establishment infects a Hologram soul version then the collateral damage could reach to the size of galaxy proportions. The only type of "Donald Trump(s)" person/people capable to stop these infected entities is God Himself and or ones who engineered that Hologram soul

Exponential Industrial Revolution: This is The Third Industrial Revolution. This revolution will produce Exponential machines. Exponential machines will be the engines that will transport individuals and individual items to whole galaxies of individuals and items anywhere in the universe at anytime; without colliding into anything anytime.

Now in a 3D world history mentality, it's easy to assume that these 3 industrial revolutions are describing what primarily happened during these point A and point B time frames. It can be trivialized to pupils learning about earth's brief recorded history, first time, as describing the time line pattern these phenomena's occurred in, but should not be water down as insignificant information. Keep in mind the generic definition of the word "revolution" is to rotate around; using the means to spin an object 360 degrees in the same spot. So we are taking things minerals/substances of the habitat we're living in and converting them into useable devices. These 3 industrial revolutions are the key components in allowing habitats on different planets to travel to "what appears as" distant galaxies. Note to the fear mongers: Why is it that when something is dark, distant and deeper than our current understanding; always considered "evil", "tyrannistical", and "death to us all" assumptions. Maybe the reason things are dark is to allow ourselves to quiet down and be at awe, then ask the question, "How can I develop a product that will allow us to lighten the darkness". It's like creating a candle on earth and lighting it at night, our homes/shelters are easier to function in, as though it was day. Maybe the reason things are distant is to allow ourselves to quiet down and be at awe, then ask the question. "How can I get there the fastest possible way physically?" It's like creating the automobile on earth and using it to get other cities in a matter of minutes versus days. Maybe the reasons things are deeper than our understanding is to allow ourselves to quiet down and be at awe, then ask the question, "How can I live in harmony with it?" *Assuming it's peaceful?*

Ok. This is a freaking awesome foundation to take this prophecy into Epic Mode…

Beyond the 3 Industrial Revolutions: After the three Industrial Revolutions have been completed; travel between galaxies will be in a blink "twinkle" of an eye. To those looking in the dark night skies, they will see them as a glimmer. As time proceeds, there will come a time when all of the creation, the exponent machines, the hologram soul machines and the physical mechanical machines will be in harmony and unity with one another within the same galaxy, so that they will be able fly/move that same/ whole galaxy anywhere in the universe in a blink of an eye. A few more galaxies will be able to accomplish the same thing. For a season, two to three galaxies will seem to be racing each other, like two automobiles on earth in the 20th century, but watching with a closer eye, one will see them flying together like two birds in a forest, with no worries.

By this time, several if not hundreds of harmonized galaxy entities, each infected with an organized network of establishments, will conspire to destroy the point of where creation was physically manifested into existence. The last phase of this conspired group of galaxies infected with an organized network of establishments, is successfully destroying the place of physical life origin, all hope is lost for everyone who is apart the universe. Including those who were apart of the beginning, those during and those in the end. No one was missing. Everyone is reflecting. Many were hanging onto what was, what is and what is to come. The whole universe ripped open like a rented fetus's placenta.

For one moment the whole universe was paralyzed in complete bone chilling silence. Knowing this was the greatest of all defining moments in all of time past, in all of time present and in all of time future.

Personal Application

How does this all apply to me?

The Donald Trump Prophecy goes to the core of what creates these life changing events. So that we can learn how to cut our lost, recycle our bad decisions and build a better life for ourselves, our families and our communities; no matter what age or century we live in.

Careers with infected entities: If I find myself employed with an entity that is infected with an establishment and if I have the flexibility of moving on, I should strongly considered it. If I continue work with this type of entity, I will more than likely have to make abrupt inconvenient changes in my life when this entity's bubble bursts. The entities that stop rewarding their senior employees are severely infected by establishments. More than likely, I will be in a stagnated job that will get meager raises until the entity's bubble bursts. The establishment is deliberately doing this to discourage me, in hopes of my departure. It is better for me to jump entities every two to three years; in this environment of multiple entities infected with establishments. The entity jumping to is more desperate in gaining skillful employees so they pay more upfront to entice skilled labor. Once employee gets the entity to where they want to be, they stop giving good raises.

Careers with non-infected entities: I will experience continual growth with respected knowledge and involvement with entities as well in my income. I will more than likely get several offers to go to other cities, and countries to establishing distribution centers, etc. I might experience the evolution of the entity increasing my wages, if not doubling them, to shift the responsibility of paying the taxes, health care and long term savings plans.

Marriage: I better off getting established in a career that pays enough for a home and transportation before getting married. This reduces the stress couples experience when starting with nothing. I marry based on the inner beauty of my companion versus their outer beauty and being socially acceptable. I marry with an age difference anywhere from five to fifteen years difference. Twenty to thirty years should be considered if the average life span is greater than 120 years old.

Family: Children heighten my enriching life experience with my companion and life itself. They help me discover and root out any hidden self-centrism within me so that I can enjoy life to its fullest with my loved ones. The larger the family the more the children will understand positive benefits of family, selflessness and companionship.

Wealth: Family is my true wealth. When I choose family over wealth then wealth will never control me.

Index

So... here we are at crossroads of another defining moment in history. Should we keep heading straight on Day Dreamers Freeway *aka DD Hwy* to Denial City? Should we take a left on Paranoia Avenue to Conspiracists Theme Park? Or should we take a right on the Real Deal Highway to Hunkerdowns Campgrounds?

Regardless of our Culture, Race and or Religion, when these major events happen, they stop us dead in our tracks and force us to make new "no turning back" life decisions.

*The President's Apocalypse prophe**cy*** goes to the core of what creates these life changing events. So that we can learn how to cut our lost, recycle our bad decisions and build a better life for ourselves, our families and our communities; no matter what age or century we live in.

Plus This Prophecy is packed with tons of additional future insights you won't find any where else on earth. Enjoy!